LISTEN '

CW01507918

Barbara Cartland

Barbara Cartland Ebooks Ltd

This edition © 2016

ISBNs

9781782137825   EPUB

9781782137832   PAPERBACK

Book design by M-Y Books
m-ybooks.co.uk

The Barbara Cartland Eternal Collection

The Barbara Cartland Eternal Collection is the unique opportunity to collect all five hundred of the timeless beautiful romantic novels written by the world's most celebrated and enduring romantic author.

Named the Eternal Collection because Barbara's inspiring stories of pure love, just the same as love itself, the books will be published on the internet at the rate of four titles per month until all five hundred are available.

The Eternal Collection, classic pure romance available worldwide for all time .

THE LATE DAME BARBARA CARTLAND

Barbara Cartland, who sadly died in May 2000 at the grand age of ninety eight, remains one of the world's most famous romantic novelists. With worldwide sales of over one billion, her outstanding 723 books have been translated into thirty six different languages, to be enjoyed by readers of romance globally.

Writing her first book 'Jigsaw' at the age of 21, Barbara became an immediate bestseller. Building upon this initial success, she wrote continuously throughout her life, producing bestsellers for an astonishing 76 years. In addition to Barbara Cartland's legion of fans in the UK and across Europe, her books have always been immensely popular in the USA. In 1976 she achieved the unprecedented feat of having books at numbers 1 & 2 in the prestigious B. Dalton Bookseller bestsellers list.

Although she is often referred to as the 'Queen of Romance', Barbara Cartland also wrote several historical biographies, six autobiographies and numerous theatrical plays as well as books on life, love, health and cookery. Becoming one of Britain's most popular media personalities and dressed in her trademark pink, Barbara spoke on radio and television about social and political issues, as well as making many public appearances.

In 1991 she became a Dame of the Order of the British Empire for her contribution to literature and her work for humanitarian and charitable causes.

Known for her glamour, style, and vitality Barbara Cartland became a legend in her own lifetime. Best remembered for her wonderful romantic novels and loved by millions of readers worldwide, her books remain treasured for their heroic heroes, plucky heroines and traditional values. But above all, it was Barbara Cartland's overriding belief in the positive power of love to help, heal and improve the quality of life for everyone that made her truly unique.

AUTHOR'S NOTE

The meaning of pianoforte (literally 'soft-loud') derives from its ability to produce gradations of volume by act of touch. In mid-eighteenth century England, it somewhat confusingly began life as a fortepiano, but the name was changed to pianoforte towards the end of the century.

Bartolommeo Cristofori (1655-1731) devised his *pravecembalo col piano è forte* in Florence in about 1709 and it is from him that the modem piano stems. But it was not until the nineteenth century development of metal bracing that the potentialities of Cristofori's remarkable action were fully realised.

Mozart first played a Stein piano in 1777 and the Viennese pianos were perfectly suited to his style of playing, a singing tone, a quiet steady hand and smoothness of execution in which passage work 'flowed like oil'.

C. P. E. Bach mentions his endeavour 'to play the pianoforte' in his *Versuch über die wahre Art das Klaviar zu Spielen*, 'despite its deficiency in sustaining tone as much as possible in a singing manner. This is by no means an easy task, if we desire not to leave the ear empty or to disturb the noble simplicity of the *cantabile* by too much noise.'

But J. C. Bach played the piano by choice and was largely responsible for popularising it in England, where he gave his first piano recital on a Zumpe Square in 1768.

After 1806 the piano, as a result of the increasing demands of composers and performers, began a rapid growth to its modem form, which, for practical purposes, it reached in 1859. The main stimulus was the gigantic pianism of Beethoven followed by the efforts of others to emulate his style and to excel in his works.

Although admired by Ravel, this clever invention seems destined to share the oblivion of any instrumental innovation that does not attract the imagination of leading composers and performers, who no doubt feel that the twentieth century grand piano is demanding enough without additional complications.

CHAPTER ONE
1817

"Anthea! Anthea!"

The name seemed to echo round the old house and Anthea, who was sorting out the sheets in the linen cupboard, started and realised with surprise that it was Harry calling her.

She put down the sheet she was holding in her hand, which, she thought regretfully was finished and there was nothing she could do about it.

Of a superfine linen it was beautifully embroidered with her father and mother's monogram and edged with crocheted lace, but Harry had put his foot through it, as he had through so many other sheets, and she realised that it was past darning or patching.

"Anthea!"

Harry's voice came again.

She thought this time that it had a distinctly urgent note in it.

She ran along the passage and, reaching the top of the ancient oak staircase, saw him standing in the hall looking, she thought, extremely handsome in his riding clothes.

But, as she hurried towards him, there was no doubt that there was a worried expression on his face, which meant, she knew, that something upsetting had happened.

"What is – it?" she asked, a little breathlessly as she reached him.

"Meldosio has hurt his hand and he cannot play tonight."

"Oh, no!" Anthea exclaimed.

"It's true," Harry said. "What the devil am I to do? How can we find someone else?"

Anthea drew a deep breath and suggested,

"Come into the drawing room and I will get you a cool drink. I can see that you are agitated."

"Of course I am agitated! What do you expect?"

He went on talking, but, without waiting to hear any more, she ran to the pantry where she had already made a fruit drink, which she hoped Harry would enjoy, knowing that it was far better for him than the claret they could not afford.

A glass jug was standing in a bowl of cold water and she wiped it, picked up a tumbler and hurried back to the drawing room.

It was a long attractive room with a ceiling of ship's beams like most of the other rooms in the old house, which had been built in Tudor times.

But, although the carpet was threadbare, surprisingly enough some of the furniture was French and valuable and so were the pictures.

Harry had thrown himself down in an armchair and his sister filled up the glass with the fruit juice and handed it to him.

He drank it without saying anything, obviously so intent on his thoughts that he did not taste what he was drinking.

A little nervously Anthea sat down on the sofa, looking at him, before she asked,

"Are you quite sure that Mr. Meldosio cannot play tonight?"

"Of course I am sure," Harry said sharply. "He cut his right hand and it is swollen to twice its normal size. He has it bandaged and it would be quite impossible for him to play the piano."

"Poor man. It must be very painful!" Anthea exclaimed.

"It's even more painful for me!" Harry said crossly. "I suppose you know this means that I may lose my job?"

"Surely it cannot be as bad as that?" Anthea protested. "It's not your fault."

"It's my fault if I don't provide what his Lordship wants," Harry said. "When he engaged me and it was the most uncomfortable interview I can ever remember, he said, 'you must understand that I always get what I want without argument and without complaint. If you cannot carry out what I require, then I will find someone else who will'."

Anthea had heard this before and she had thought then that the Marquis of Eaglescliffe was an extremely unpleasant man and her conviction that he was overbearing and undoubtedly a bully had increased ever since.

In the meantime she was well aware that for Harry to lose the position of manager of what had once been his own estate would be a tragedy.

It seemed almost providential when, owing to the immense debts left by their father on his death, after much heart-searching and misery Harry had decided that he must sell the house, Queen's Hoo, and much of the land that went with it.

His friend, Charlie Torrington, had found a purchaser who would not only pay what seemed to be an astronomical sum for Queen's Hoo, but would also employ Harry to manage the house and the estate for him.

"I have it all fixed up, old boy," he had said jubilantly when he had posted from London to bring Harry the good news. "I am bringing Eaglescliffe down on Wednesday to inspect the house, although he has already decided to buy it from the description I gave him."

"*Eaglescliffe*! The Marquis of Eaglescliffe!" Harry had ejaculated. "What on earth does he want with Queen's Hoo? After all his own ancestral mansion is one of the most spectacular and famous in the whole country."

"Of course it is," Charlie agreed. "But, as you well know, it's in Oxfordshire and it takes him, even with his superb horses, a long time to get there from London, while he is banking on reaching Queen's Hoo in under the hour."

"But he has also the house in Berkeley Square in London," Harry said. "I still don't understand why he should want to live here."

"It is not a question of living, you idiot!" Charlie laughed. "He wants somewhere to bring his latest fancy for a weekend or a night or two. At the moment she is Lottie Vernon, who is a ballet dancer at *Covent Garden*. He can hardly take her to Eaglescliffe Castle."

Harry stiffened.

"I am not sure I want my home," he said sharply, "to be turned into a kind of upper class brothel."

Charlie had thrown out his hands.

"My dear Harry, you cannot afford to be particular. You are well aware that the sum Eaglescliffe is prepared to pay will cover your father's debts, pension off the old servants, who have been a great anxiety to you these last months and leave enough to feed you and your sister. If you take the position I suggest, you will, in fact, be very comfortable."

"Position! What position?" Harry had asked.

"You cannot accuse me, old boy, of not thinking of you," Charlie said, "for I know how you would hate to see someone else running what has been your estate and very likely doing it badly."

He saw from the expression on his friend's face that he had hit the nail on the head.

"The noble Marquis," he went on, "has told me to find him a manager and he thought a local man would very likely be more efficient than someone from outside."

Harry, who had been listening, sat up in his chair, and looked at his friend in astonishment as Charlie continued,

"I therefore told him that I had just the right man in view – keen, intelligent, absolutely honest and trustworthy. Name of Dalton."

"Dalton?" Harry questioned.

"That's you! Don't be bird-witted, Harry! I have set all this up and it has taken me a great deal of time, I may tell you. So I expect you to be grateful."

"I am. You know I am, Charlie," Harry said, "but I am finding it hard to understand what exactly is happening."

"What is happening," Charlie replied, "is that I am repaying the debt that I have owed you since the Battle of Waterloo when you saved my life."

"Oh, that!" Harry exclaimed scornfully.

"It meant quite a lot to me," Charlie said with a grin. "Now, as I cannot bear to see you down in the dumps as you have been ever since your father died, I have found the solution. You sell Queen's Hoo and the estate for a great deal more than it is worth and you manage it. From all you have told me, it needs a great deal of managing after years of neglect."

"That is true," Harry reflected, "but – "

"No buts about it, old boy," Charlie Torrington interposed. "The fact that I have brought Eaglescliffe up to scratch and convinced him that Queen's Hoo is exactly what he wants at the moment, has been, in my opinion, a miracle."

He paused before he went on,

"He is prepared to spend a fortune on the house. You know damn well that is exactly what it needs. The last time I stayed here the water dripped through the ceiling all night and I caught the worst cold I have had in years."

Harry had risen from the chair where he was sitting to walk to the window and stand, with unseeing eyes, looking out at the unkempt overgrown garden.

Charlie Torrington watched him sympathetically. He knew how much it was going to hurt Harry to sell Queen's Hoo, which had been in his family since the time of Queen Elizabeth.

It was exceedingly beautiful, but, as the late Lord Colnbrooke had been unable to find any money for repairs, the roof leaked, the ceilings were cracked, dozens of the diamond-paned windows needed replacing and in nearly every room floorboards creaked ominously when they were walked on.

Besides this, as Harry well knew, there was not enough money to pay any servants or even for the food he and his sister ate.

At the same time to part with his home in which his family had lived since Elizabethan times was a wrench that Charlie knew would make Harry feel as if he was losing a leg or an arm.

There was silence until Harry said gruffly,

"When does the Marquis wish to move in?"

"As soon as the place is made comfortable enough for him," Charlie replied. "Knowing Eaglescliffe, I expect that means tomorrow."

"That is impossible at any rate," Harry remarked.

Charlie walked across the room to put his arm across his friend's shoulders.

"Now, listen, Harry," he said. "I know this upsets you, but the person who is going to supervise the repairs, the alterations, the renovations and make the house look as if it is new, is you."

"Me!" Harry exclaimed in amazement.

"Who else?" Charlie asked. "That is why in a twisted sort of way you are going to enjoy yourself. This will mean you will see Queen's Hoo as it once looked in all its glory and you have always said that you and your sister would sooner or later have to move into the Dower House because the roof would cave in over your heads!"

That was true enough, but even Harry had not anticipated, although, of course, he had heard of him and seen him, what the Marquis of Eaglescliffe was like.

He had swept down to Queen's Hoo the next day, with Charlie sitting beside him, in a phaeton drawn by four horses, which made Harry green with envy.

The phaeton was also the smartest carriage he had ever imagined could be propelled on four wheels and, as the Marquis descended from it, he knew that no man could be so impressive or look so extremely smart.

He looked at Queen's Hoo in an almost contemptuous manner, which made Harry hate him.

"Is this the house?" he had asked, as if, as Harry said to Charlie afterwards, it was a pigsty.

"I thought you would admire it, my Lord," Charlie answered cheerfully. "It's the finest bit of Tudor architecture in the whole county and, as you can imagine, it is named Queen's Hoo because Queen Elizabeth slept here."

"Among a hundred other places," the Marquis added sarcastically.

"If this was Her Majesty's choice, I don't blame her," Charlie said. "Although, as I warned you, it wants a lot doing to it, you cannot help seeing tremendous possibilities in restoring it."

The Marquis did not reply, but walked into the hall with its oak staircase and great carved stone fireplace in which, as Charlie pointed out, a whole tree could be burnt.

He then moved into the drawing room with its windows overlooking an ancient Rose Garden and paused for a moment to look at a portrait of a beautiful Lady Colnbrooke, who was reputed to have fascinated King Charles II.

"Are these family portraits?" he asked.

"Yes, all of them," Charlie said quickly. "Naturally they would not be included in the sale, but I am sure if there is anything else your Lordship fancies, Lord Colnbrooke would be prepared to discuss selling it."

He was well aware that Harry, who had been introduced as Mr. Dalton, was behind him and had stiffened as the Marquis spoke.

The Marquis looked disdainfully at everything he saw including the ancient library with its walls covered with leather-bound books, their covers faded and torn with age, and it was obvious that he was not interested in them.

Only when he had seen every room on the ground floor including the Chapel and the State Rooms on the first floor, where the curtains of the beds and the windows were in tatters, did he say scathingly,

"You are certainly asking an exorbitant sum for very little."

"It does not include the contents," Charlie replied instantly, "but I know that your Lordship with your knowledge of architecture is appreciating the fine proportions of the rooms themselves and, of course, of the outside, while the setting of the house is unique."

The Marquis did not reply and Harry, listening, was quite certain that he would either call the whole deal off or beat Charlie down with regard to the price he was asking for it.

Unpredictably, which was characteristic of him, the Marquis did none of those things.

He merely walked back into the hall, told Harry that he would engage him on Major Charles Torrington's recommendation with the proviso that if he was not satisfactory he must be prepared to leave at a moment's notice.

"Let me make it quite clear, Dalton," he said in his hard voice, "I expect perfection and I intend to have it!"

"I will do my best, my Lord, to satisfy you," Harry said with difficulty.

He was finding it hard to play a subservient part while his house was sold over his head and the man who was buying it appeared to find everything about it distasteful.

Then the Marquis said unexpectedly,

"I understand that you served with Major Torrington in the Household Brigade at the Battle of Waterloo."

"Yes, my Lord," Harry answered.

"A great battle," the Marquis said reflectively, "and I want you to show the same intelligence, the same initiative and the same efficiency if you work for me. Do you understand?"

"I understand," Harry said quietly.

"Very well then, I will engage you," the Marquis went on, "and my orders are to put the restoration of this house in hand immediately. My secretary will come down from London tomorrow to see you and make sure you have available all the money that is necessary. I shall expect a report from you each month as to how things are progressing. It is essential that the work should be completed as quickly as possible."

As he finished speaking, he walked towards the front door, saying in a casual manner as he did so,

"Are you coming back with me, Torrington, or do you still intend to stay?"

"I would rather stay, if you don't mind," Charlie replied. "I hope to see Lord Colnbrooke, who, as I have already told you, is extremely sorry that he could not be here to meet you today. I want to tell him exactly what has been decided and I am sure he will be very grateful."

The Marquis did not deign to reply, but climbed back into his phaeton, picked up the reins and drove off, looking so magnificent as he did so that both Harry and Charlie watched him without speaking until he was out of sight.

Then Charlie had given a little whoop of excitement.

"We have done it, Harry!" he said. "He has bought it! I never for a moment dreamt he would pay what I asked for it."

"You don't think he will change his mind?" Harry said in a low voice.

"He prides himself on his reputation that once he has given his word he never goes back on it," Charlie answered. "No, Harry, the money is yours and so is the position of manager, although you are going to find it damned hard work."

That was certainly true and only Anthea knew how many hours Harry worked, and so did she, during the next weeks.

First they had to get the Dower House, which was almost in the same state as Queen's Hoo, habitable, and then they had to move in all the things they could from the Big House.

It was quite impossible to take everything because the Dower House was quite small, with only five bedrooms besides those supposed to be occupied by servants, three sitting rooms and the dining hall.

It was actually an exceedingly attractive little house, where a series of Dowager Lady Colnbrookes had spent happily the last years of their lives.

At the same time Anthea, like Harry, knew it would never mean the same to them as Queen's Hoo. However dilapidated, however dusty, threadbare and ragged their home looked, they loved it.

They loved the huge staircase with its polished bannisters down which they had slid as children, the long corridors with innumerable rooms opening out of them and the history that belonged to every nook and cranny of the house with its priests' hole, secret staircases, ghosts, and dungeons and on winter nights Anthea was sure that she could hear the cries of the prisoners incarcerated there.

Her father had always laughed and said they were not really dungeons but hidden cellars in which, doubtless, Protestants under the tyranny of Mary Tudor had hidden and later Catholics under Queen Elizabeth, who had heretics burnt at the stake.

If they were not hiding places, Lord Colnbrooke had continued with them and then later they might easily have harboured contraband for smugglers who came up the Thames and were in touch with quite a number of large landowners round London, who were prepared to pay huge sums for French wines and especially brandy.

But Anthea thought of those dark, cold airless little rooms as dungeons and would never go into them if she could help it.

Everywhere else in the house she and Harry had romped and hidden, jumping out at each other from secret doors in the panelling and frightening the servants by pretending that they were ghosts.

Now, Anthea thought miserably, there would be strange people living in the rooms where her mother had sat and a new owner sleeping in the bedroom where her father had slept and where every Head of the Family had slept before him.

The more she thought about the Marquis the more she hated him, although she had tried to tell herself that it was unchristian and that she should be grateful to him for giving Harry the money he needed so badly.

Yet she was sure that he was an overbearing ruthless man who had no sympathy or understanding of other people.

Harry had not told her the reason that the Marquis was buying Queen's Hoo, as explained to him by Charlie, but she was suspicious that something strange was happening.

After the house was completed, and she had to admit that the workmen had done a wonderful job on it and so had Harry in directing and supervising them, she learnt that the Marquis was intending to celebrate his arrival as its new owner by giving a party.

"They will not stay long," she heard Charlie say to her brother when he did not know that she was listening. "Lottie will have to be back at the theatre by Monday evening. But I understand she has a small dancing part on Saturday night, so they will all be here in time for dinner."

Although she lived in the country and knew nothing about London, Anthea had heard Harry speak of Lottie Vernon as a superlative dancer and he and

Charlie admired her, as apparently did all the young men who frequented the Clubs in St. James's.

"Eaglescliffe has given her jewels to make her shine like a Christmas tree," Anthea heard Charlie say on another occasion.

She thought it strange that the Marquis should spend so much money on an actress, but she supposed that he was, in fact, a great admirer of her talent.

It meant perhaps no more than another man giving her a bouquet of flowers, she told herself. She remembered how her father had said ballerinas and opera singers always received immense bouquets after their performances and would have been very upset if they had been neglected by their admirers.

At the same time Harry's behaviour and the way he spoke about the party to Charlie made her realise that he was nervous.

Charlie spent much of his time coming down to the Dower House to tell Harry what was happening in London and Anthea knew that he was trying to make up to him for the excitements he was missing while forced by his new duties to stay in the country.

Not that Harry minded, his only anxiety being to do everything that the Marquis wanted and avoid being dismissed from his position as manager, which, as Charlie had anticipated, was definitely a compensation for no longer being the owner.

She had to admit to herself that it was fascinating to watch the house growing more beautiful day by day.

Having unlimited money to spend, Harry had been able to engage all the bricklayers, the carpenters, the plasterers and the painters within miles of Queen's Hoo. They arrived early in the morning in large brakes drawn by two horses and were taken home in the same way at night.

Anthea was very proud that Harry appeared so efficient at doing something he had never done before.

Of course as a soldier he had been accustomed to giving orders and expected them to be obeyed, but she knew also that Harry had the same charm that her father had had and the workmen tried their best to please him.

They actually enjoyed their work in a way that they would not have done under a different sort of overseer.

As Harry, owing to the war, had been away from home for several years, the majority of these workmen, not knowing him by sight, were unaware that he was, in reality, Lord Colnbrooke.

Anthea thought it very unlikely, from what she had heard of the Marquis, that he would trouble himself to visit the retired pensioners living in the village or anyone else who had known Harry since he was a child and were likely to give him away.

"I only hope that I remember to answer to 'Dalton'," Harry had said with a grin soon after starting work on Queen's Hoo. "Whatever made you choose that name, Charlie?"

"I once had a tutor called 'Dalton'," Charlie replied, "a tiresome sort of chap, but rather good at his job and I thought the name would suit you!"

"You might have asked me before you rechristened me," Harry complained.

"There was no time, my dear boy," Charlie replied. "I was thinking about you in White's Club, when Eaglescliffe happened to come into the Club and somebody said in a whisper,

"'Here comes Midas and, what is more, he made a packet at the races yesterday. Money always goes to money!'

"He spoke rather bitterly, but it suddenly struck me that here was exactly the person you wanted for Queen's Hoo."

Harry said nothing and Anthea, thinking that he sounded ungrateful, said quickly,

"You have been very very kind, Charlie, and you know that we could not have gone on as we were."

Charles had looked at her as if he saw her for the first time. He had known her, of course, for years, but she was five years younger than her brother and he had grown used to thinking of her as a child.

Now he realised that she had grown, while he was away fighting the French, into a very attractive young woman. In fact 'lovely' was the word, he thought to himself, he would use to describe her.

Yet there was still something very child-like about her blue eyes, which were the colour of the thrush's egg. They were so clear and innocent that he knew she must not come into contact with Eaglescliffe.

He waited until she was out of the room and then said to Harry in a low voice,

"Whatever you do, Harry, don't let the Marquis come here or meet Anthea."

Harry looked surprised.

"Why not?"

"Don't be a fool!" Charlie said. "You know what he is like with women and Anthea, although I have only just realised it, has grown very pretty lately."

"Has she?" Harry asked vaguely.

He was so used to his sister running after him, virtually fagging for him as small boys at Eton had fagged for him during his last term, that it was hard to think of her except with her fair hair tumbling untidily over her shoulders, her dress torn and her white socks crumpled around her ankles.

Now, when she came back into the room, he looked at her and realised that, although she was badly dressed, she had a grace that he had not noticed before and her face, though it still looked very young, was not exactly that of a child.

That night, when he went to say 'good night' to her as he usually did, he sat down on the edge of the bed and said,

"Listen, Anthea, Charlie was telling me today that, when the Marquis comes down at the end of the week, you are not to meet him."

Anthea laughed.

"I never thought I should. Are you expecting him to invite me to dinner?"

"No, of course not," Harry answered quickly. "I was only thinking that while he is in residence you must not go riding or walking in the Park and, of course, on no account are you to go to Queen's Hoo."

"I know what is worrying you," Anthea said. "Because we rather resemble each other, he might, if he sees me, be suspicious that you are not Mr. Dalton."

Harry had accepted this explanation with relief.

"Yes, of course," he agreed. "That is what I was thinking and therefore you must be very careful. To put it bluntly, keep out of sight!"

"To hear, O Master, is to obey!" Anthea teased him. "But I shall have to have a little peep at him sometime, somehow. You know that I have never seen the Marquis."

"You are not to see him!" Harry said sharply. "You quite understand, Anthea, you are to stay here and, if by any chance he comes to the door, you are to make it clear to Nanny that you are not at home."

Anthea lay back against her pillows and laughed.

"You are making me more and more curious about him."

"You are not to be curious," Harry said. "Make no mistake, Anthea, he is a very unpleasant man with a shocking reputation. If there had been any other possible purchaser of Queen's Hoo, I would not under any circumstances have sold it to the Marquis."

"I cannot believe that many rich men were tumbling over themselves to buy the house," Anthea said. "So I am grateful, Harry, that we are not encumbered with Papa's debts for the rest of our lives."

She paused for a moment, aware that her brother was frowning, and went on,

"I went to see poor old Burrows today and he is so thrilled at the way you have done up the cottage for him.

'I've never been so comfortable in me whole life, Miss Anthea,' he said. It made me happy to see him."

"Thank God I could do something for the pensioners," Harry murmured.

"And Nanny is thrilled," Anthea went on, "that you have given her a lump sum to make up for all the years she was paid no wages. 'Now I can pay for my funeral,' she said to me, but I told her that, if she died, it would be very inconvenient for us and very unkind of her."

"It certainly would," Harry smiled.

He was thinking as he spoke that Nanny was a better chaperone than anyone else he could find for Anthea.

He had already spoken to her about his sister and Nanny had said firmly,

"Now don't you go worryin' yourself, Master Harry. I'll go on lookin' after Miss Anthea, as I always have, and from what I've heard of his Lordship, there's none of it in his favour."

Her voice sharpened as she continued,

"And bringin' those vulgar women from the theatre down here is not my idea of how a gentleman should behave. Your dear mother would turn in her grave!"

"Don't talk about it in front of Anthea, Nanny," Harry had begged. "You will only make her curious and then she will want to see the Marquis just because she has no idea of what a man of that sort looks like."

"I'll see she stays here with me, Master Harry – I mean, my Lord," Nanny replied.

Harry rose from the kitchen table where he had been sitting.

"I am not 'my Lord' to you, Nanny. I am Mr. Dalton and please don't forget it."

He went from the kitchen as he spoke, but not before he had heard Nanny say with a sniff,

"Mr. Dalton, indeed! What's the world comin' to, I'd like to know, when a man is afraid to use his rightful name?"

In the months he had been restoring Queen's Hoo, repainting the rooms and the ceilings, constructing an entirely new kitchen with up to date stoves and spits that shone like polished silver, Harry had seen the Marquis a number of times when he came down to inspect what was happening and to insist that things should be done more quickly.

He had also gone to London on one occasion to make his monthly report and to be told firmly and briefly that the Marquis did not intend to wait any longer.

"I bought the house for a certain purpose, Dalton," he had said in his clear imperious voice, "and it is now getting towards the summer. I want to be here in the country next Saturday and Sunday, since there will not be time to take the guests I wish to have with me elsewhere."

He rapped the table with a ruler before he continued,

"You are therefore to finish the main bedrooms of the house. Stock the whole place with servants, whom I trust you to engage, although my secretary will help if you have any difficulties and I intend to arrive with a party on Saturday, May 20th."

"It's rather soon, my Lord," Harry had said desperately.

"Not soon enough for me," the Marquis replied. "I am bringing with me not only Miss Lottie Vernon, of whom, of course, you have heard, but several attractive young ballet dancers from Covent Garden, who will give us a performance during dinner."

"A performance, my Lord?" Harry gasped.

"It's quite easy," the Marquis continued. "You will erect a small stage about eighteen inches high under the Minstrels' Gallery in the Dining Hall. The girls will do their *poses plastiques*, which is one of the new forms of entertainment that has arrived from the Continent. All they will need is a pianist and I wish you to find one for me locally."

He thought that Harry had looked surprised and he then explained,

"The girls from the ballet will all be looked after by my particular friends and a pianist whom they knew would be an embarrassment. That is why you must find one who will play and then leave. Do you understand?"

"Yes, of course, my Lord," Harry agreed.

The Marquis thought for a moment and then added,

"While I think of it, it would be nice to have music during dinner. Soft gentle music that would not interfere with the conversation, but make the atmosphere in that rather over-large Dining Hall rather more congenial. You will therefore instruct the man to play in the Minstrels' Gallery and then come downstairs when we reach the dessert, when the performers will start immediately on the stage you have constructed. For their performance, I understand, all that is wanted is an accompaniment of music to which the girls can do their postures. Now, is that clear?"

"I am sure I can arrange it, my Lord," Harry answered. "We have locally an accomplished pianist who retired after he had some trouble with his heart. But he is an excellent player and I am sure that he would be delighted to accommodate your Lordship for a small fee."

"Give him whatever he asks," the Marquis ordered. "Don't bother me with details, just see that everything is arranged as I want it and that the stage is properly draped and, of course, decorated with flowers."

"Naturally, my Lord."

On the way back from London Harry stopped at Mr. Meldosio's little house, which was more imposing than a cottage, but still very small, on the outskirts of the village.

A good-looking man of Italian extraction with hair that was now white, he lived comfortably with his sister, who looked after him, and spent much of his time enjoying an aviary of small birds, which he had acquired over the years.

He greeted Harry with delight.

"This is an unexpected surprise, Lord Colnbrooke," he said. "I have not seen you for so long, I thought you had forgotten me."

"I expect you have heard that I have been busy at Queen's Hoo," Harry replied.

Mr. Meldosio's eyes twinkled.

"I have indeed. I understand that now you are Mr. Dalton and the manager."

"Exactly," Harry replied. "I want your help on Saturday night and I shall be very disappointed if you refuse."

Mr. Meldosio, however, was delighted to oblige.

"It will be like old times," he said. "Although my fingers are a little stiff in the morning, I exercise them every day and I don't think that Miss Lottie Vernon will be disappointed in me."

"I am sure that she will admire your music, as we all do," Harry said.

He drove on home to tell Anthea what he had arranged.

Now, as she sat looking at her brother, she realised only too well what a disaster it would be if he disappointed the Marquis the very first night on his arrival at Queen's Hoo.

It was now Friday morning and, even if Harry rode into the nearest town, she doubted if he would find anyone as proficient as Mr. Meldosio and there was no time for auditions or rehearsals.

Harry put his empty glass down with a bang on the table beside him.

"What can I do, Anthea?" he asked. "What the devil can I do?"

"It's quite easy. I know the answer. I can play for you."

Harry stared at her as if she had taken leave of her senses.

"You! Of course not! Don't be silly!"

"You know," Anthea replied, "I can play the piano, not as well as Mr. Meldosio, but very well. Well enough to please Papa and he said once that, if I ever had to earn my living, he was certain that with a lot of practice I would be up to professional standard."

"He was just flattering you!" Harry said.

But even as he spoke, he knew that his sister was an exceedingly good player and a great number of people had told him how moved they were by her music.

She played the organ in Church every Sunday and, although he thought himself unmusical, he knew that out of the rickety old organ, which should have been replaced years ago, Anthea could extract sounds that might have come from the angels themselves.

All this flashed through his mind, until suddenly he thought of the Marquis and exclaimed,

"It's impossible! Utterly impossible!"

"Very well," said Anthea. "You find someone else." She looked at the clock over the mantelpiece and said, "It is now nearly noon. It gives you about eight hours to find someone."

Harry groaned.

"You know I have not got time to look anywhere. There are a million things still to be done up at the house. The gardeners are bringing the flowers in and I have to see that they are arranged properly. When I left this morning the curtains that I ordered for the stage had not been hung and, if I don't supervise the

~27~

decoration of the dining table, it will be a mess. Williams is a good gardener, but his artistic sense is about that of a rabbit."

He spoke in an agitated way and Anthea said soothingly,

"Of course, dearest, I understand. It's much easier to let me play than to worry yourself to try to find someone who does not exist in the short time you have available."

"You know I cannot allow you to be in touch with the Marquis and his friends."

"They are not likely to eat me," Anthea replied, "and quite frankly, Harry, though I appreciate the compliment, I cannot believe that I compare with Lottie Vernon!"

This was undeniable, Harry thought.

He looked at his sister, who was now wearing a cotton gown that was faded from endless washings, her hair straggling a little untidily round her face and he told himself that never in a thousand years would the Marquis be likely to be interested in this country girl when he was already obsessed by the most exotic and alluring ballet dancer in the whole of London.

As if she knew that he was weakening, Anthea sat on the arm of her brother's chair and put her arm round his neck.

"Listen, dearest," she said, "I know that you are worried about me and it is very sweet of you. But I promise you, on my honour, that I will behave sensibly. I will just play what is expected of me and then return home as quickly as possible with Nanny."

"You will bring Nanny with you?"

Harry seized on the idea as if it was a lifeline in a very rough sea.

"Yes, of course. Nanny can wait in the housekeeper's room. She certainly knows where that is. And the moment I have finished playing I will come home with her. It will not take more than ten minutes to walk across the Park."

There was silence and then Harry said,

"I am sure that I am doing the wrong thing! I am sure that I should refuse to listen to you, but I cannot afford to give up my job and quite frankly I don't want to."

"No, of course not!"

"It has been a great satisfaction," he went on, "to be able to do exactly what I wanted for the farmers who struggled on all through the War without hope and without, as one man told me, anyone to repair a cowshed for him."

"I know, I know!" Anthea said. "And they are very grateful, Harry. Mrs. Barnes told me only two days ago that you were like St. Michael himself coming down from Heaven to save them from utter ruin."

Harry grinned.

"She should really be thanking the Marquis, as you well know. I will say this for him, he has never queried any of my expenses where it has concerned the farms, the pensioners or anything else on the estate – "

"He cannot be as bad as he is painted," Anthea said.

"Yes, he is!" Harry insisted. "He is a bad man and make no mistake about it, I will not have you knowing him or talking to him. Do you understand, Anthea? You will hide yourself from the moment you have to play. And as soon as the performance is over, you and Nanny will leave Queen's Hoo and come back here."

"I promise that is what I will do."

"And what is more," Harry went on, "concentrate on your music and don't look at or listen to anything else. I will not have you polluted by the riff-raff that the Marquis chooses to bring, as he has no right to do, into my house."

Anthea wanted to point out that it was no longer Harry's house, but she thought that it would be unkind.

Instead of which, she kissed her brother's cheek and said,

"Don't worry, Harry, everything will be all right. I am sure that the Marquis will be quite satisfied with my playing, but will not be in the least curious about a mere pianist."

"Probably not," Harry agreed.

But Anthea knew from the way he spoke that he was still worried, although she told herself that quite unexpectedly and very excitingly this, in her quiet uneventful life, was an adventure.

chapter two

The Marquis left London in a bad temper.

If there was one thing he really disliked more than anything else, it was when his plans went wrong.

He had, in fact, taken a great deal of trouble in arranging this particular party in the country.

The first thing to arrange was that the ballet on Saturday night at *Covent Garden* should not be one in which Lottie Vernon played such a large part that it could not be taken by an understudy.

This was not as difficult as it sounded because the Marquis had financed a number of the *Covent Garden* shows and, since as a patron he was respected, no one had any desire to offend him.

In the ballet therefore that was to be given on Saturday, Lottie would have had only a small part, the most important one being that of a male dancer.

The Marquis then invited his party with the same care and attention that he gave to everything he undertook.

The men were all his special friends and rivals on the Racecourse, in his Club and at the shooting parties that they ALL enjoyed in the autumn.

Five of them were members of the same hunt as the Marquis and invariably spent some time in the winter staying with him at his hunting lodge in Leicestershire.

As regards the women, he had taken Lottie's advice in asking three of the young *Convent Garden* ballet dancers recently arrived from France, who were, she assured him, expert in the *poses plastiques*, which had become exceedingly popular in Paris.

The Marquis was sure that if their performance was anything like as exotic and unusual as he had seen the last time he had been to the 'Gay City,' his friends who had not been so fortunate would be entranced by it.

There was therefore to be a good sprinkling from *Covent Garden* in his party and by exercising his authority he managed to ensure that not only Lottie but also the ballerinas she advised him to invite would not be required on stage on Saturday night.

The rest of the women were the choice of his friends, several of whom were keeping a 'fair Cyprian' in very much the same style as he accorded Lottie.

It was, of course, only to be expected that Lottie's house was larger and more extravagantly furnished and the carriage and horses he provided her with eclipsed those of every 'bit of muslin' in the whole of London.

As he drove his phaeton to Chelsea, the Marquis was thinking of how well he managed his comfort where women were concerned.

Equally he was looking forward to being with Lottie at Queen's Hoo without what was to him the aggravation of having to rise in the early hours of the morning to return to his own house in Berkeley Square.

It was something that he was beginning to find irksome in conducting his social *affaires de coeur*, when it was a question of leaving the house long before there was any chance of an early rising housemaid being about who would gossip in a way that might eventually reach the ears of her Master.

"I am tired," the Marquis remembered saying to one charmer, whose beauty had inflamed him so that the hours of darkness had seemed to flash by as their passion appeared insatiable.

"I know, darling," she had replied. "At the same time, while the night-footman is entirely reliable because you tip him so generously, I don't trust anyone else not to chatter about us. I half-suspect that my mother-in-law's abominable nosey lady's maid is trying to find out something that will discredit me."

The Marquis had therefore risen from a warm comfortable bed to dress himself, which he could do exceedingly well without the aid of a valet.

He had then gone out into the cold night air, where his closed carriage manned by a yawning coachman and a sleepy footman was waiting for him.

'Tonight,' he told himself, 'I can enjoy myself without having to keep one eye on the clock.'

As he spoke, he turned his horses into the attractive avenue that stood in front of the Royal

Hospital built by Charles II at the request of his mistress, Nell Gwynne.

The trees that lined the sides of the road were covered with their spring leaves and the sunshine made the windows of the houses glitter and increased their attraction.

The Marquis had taken great trouble to ensure his own comfort before he installed Lottie Vernon in a house he had bought a year before he met her for another of his mistresses who had proved unsatisfactory.

While he had allowed Lottie to choose the decoration for her bedroom in what he privately considered bad taste, he installed for himself a bathroom that aroused the admiration and astonishment of everyone she showed it to.

Harry had been equally astonished when the Marquis had instructed him that every one of the powder-closets at Queen's Hoo, and there were five of them all connecting with the State bedrooms, were to be converted into bathrooms.

"Bathrooms, my Lord?" he had questioned, feeling that he could not have heard the Marquis aright.

Then, when he had seen how delightful the first one looked, he had told Anthea that he was going to have a bathroom installed in the Dower House.

She had been as surprised as he had been when he received the Marquis's order.

"Why do we want a bathroom?" she asked.

"Because it is going to save an immense amount of labour, in our case mine, in carrying cans of water upstairs," he replied.

Anthea had known that this was true. Jacobs, the odd-job man who looked after the garden at the Dower House, brought in the wood and coal for the fires and carried away the rubbish.

He also took the heavy brass cans of water upstairs in the morning for Harry's bath, which he took in a tub in his bedroom.

Harry, however, carried the hot water up for his sister because she usually bathed in the evening, when old Jacobs had disappeared into the tiny cottage he occupied at the end of the stable yard.

Even Nanny was unwilling to call Jacobs out again after a hard day's work.

Harry had been very good-humoured about it, but at the same time he himself was quite prepared to bathe in cold water in the morning and at night, except when it was so cold that he had to break the ice to do so.

"If we have a bathroom," he said to Anthea, "it will make everything very much easier. If you don't believe me, come and look at the one that has just been finished at Queen's Hoo."

"I have every intention of doing that," Anthea answered, "but it seems a very strange thing to want when we have always bathed in our bedrooms."

However, as soon as she saw the bathrooms, she was entranced.

To begin with, they opened out of the bedrooms themselves, which meant a lady would not have to be seen in the passages in her dressing gown, which would have shocked her mother.

Secondly, she had never imagined anything so attractive as the Marquis's bath, which, unlike all the others, was sunk into the floor in what Harry told her proudly was Roman fashion, where instead of climbing into a bath, one walked down into it.

From the moment she had seen it, Anthea was as excited as Harry at the idea of having a bath at the Dower House.

"I'll still have to heat all the hot water you need on this rusty old stove," Nanny had grumbled, "and if the bath's bigger than the tub you are usin' already, all I can say is, you won't get it hot."

Nanny's grumbles were appeased when, buying the new stoves for Queen's Hoo, Harry bought one for the Dower House as well.

When Charles Torrington saw it, he laughed and said,

"You may as well make yourselves comfortable at the Marquis's expense."

Harry glared at him.

"I paid for it myself out of my own money," he said. "You gave me a reference, Charlie, for being honest and trustworthy and that is what I have every intention of being."

Charlie apologised.

At the same time Anthea could not help hoping that the Marquis was aware of how scrupulous his new manager, Mr. Dalton, was about such things.

She knew that every improvement he made at the Dower House Harry paid for out of the money he had received from the Marquis for the sale of Queen's Hoo.

She thought, as Charlie had, that it would have been very easy to slip a little extra onto the enormous bills that went back to London for the renovation of the Big House.

But Harry had said to her,

"I may have to work for my living, but I am still a gentleman and have no intention of forgetting that fact."

*

The Marquis as he drew up outside his house in Royal Avenue was not thinking particularly of the bathroom he used when he visited Lottie Vernon but rather that everything in the house was arranged to his satisfaction.

With the exception of Lottie's maid, who was also her dresser at the theatre, a woman for whom he had no liking, the resident maidservants had been chosen by his secretary, Mr. Cunningham.

On the nights that he dined with Lottie, his second chef and first footman went ahead to make sure that the food was to his liking and he was waited on in the same way as he was in Berkeley Square.

In the cellar beneath the house there were crates of the special champagne, claret and port that he habitually drank and regularly every week, eggs, chickens, fruit and vegetables came up from the country, so that there was little to buy from the shops in London.

The Marquis brought his team of horses, which were perfectly matched and which he had bought from Tattersalls at the beginning of the year, to a standstill.

The groom quickly jumped down from the back of the phaeton, where he had been sitting on a small seat, to go to the horses' heads.

The Marquis, taking his time, descended.

He was looking exceedingly elegant and his Hessian boots, decorated with gold tassels in the front, shone so brilliantly that they seemed to mirror the sunshine and the railings as he walked up to the front door.

As he expected, it opened before he had need to touch the silver knocker, for the simple reason that he had sent a footman to the house a few hours earlier to tell them the precise time at which he was arriving.

Lottie's dresser, Sarah, stood in the open doorway and, as the Marquis would have walked past her, she said,

"Bad news, my Lord. Miss Lottie's ill."

The Marquis stopped.

"Did you say ill?" he questioned.

"Yes, my Lord, taken bad, she was, last night when we gets 'ome after the performance. Now she can't 'ardly speak nor move her 'ead from the pillow."

"Why did you not let me know?" the Marquis enquired.

Sarah, who was an ugly middle-aged woman with the suspicion of a squint, shrugged her shoulders.

"I keeps thinkin' she'd get better, knowin' how upset you'd be if she couldn't come, as you wanted. Instead, she's worse."

"Have you sent for a doctor?"

"Yes. He comes about midday. Says she's got Spring Fever and there's lots of other people as 'ave it too."

The Marquis thought that he had heard enough and, without saying another word, walked up the small staircase to Lottie's room.

It occupied almost the whole of the first floor and was a riot of pink satin, muslin curtains edged with lace, and, what was fortunately the Marquis's contribution, an Aubusson carpet.

In the centre of the very large bed beneath the lace- edged curtains which fell from a golden corolla of dancing angels, Lottie was lying with her dark hair streaming over the pillows, her eyes closed.

She certainly, the Marquis thought at a first glance, looked ill, without any make-up to alleviate the pallor of her face.

When she opened her eyes slowly as he reached the end of the bed, he thought that they were swollen.

"I'm sorry," she said weakly, "but I feel like hell!"

"Has the doctor given you anything to make you better?" the Marquis asked.

"Some filthy stuff that tastes like dishwater!" Lottie replied. "And it doesn't stop me from coughing."

The effort of speaking brought on a paroxysm of coughing that seemed to shake her whole body.

The Marquis waited until she collapsed back against the pillows and then he said,

"I will tell my own doctor to visit you and you must certainly not get up when you are in such a condition."

"I'm sure I'll be able to dance on Monday," Lottie murmured.

Leaving the room, the Marquis thought that did not help what he thought of as his ruined party.

He, however, drove back to Berkeley Square, told his secretary to send his doctor, who also attended the Prince Regent, to see Lottie and instructed Mr. Cunningham to have a basket of orchids delivered to the house in Royal Avenue as soon as possible.

It annoyed him intensely to know, as he drove away, that the numbers of his house party were now odd instead of even and, while everyone else had been carefully paired, he would be odd man out and it was too late now to fill Lottie's place with anybody else.

He thought, and it made him more irritated than he was already, that she had deliberately not informed him earlier in the day that she would be unable to come with him to the country.

Although it was the sort of jealous action he expected, it did not make him any more pleased at the prospect of his careful plan for the inauguration of Queen's Hoo being upset.

He had, although he had no intention of admitting it to Dalton, been delighted at the way in which the house had seemed to blossom and come to life almost fantastically every time he saw it.

He knew that Charles Torrington had not exaggerated when he had said that it was indisputably one of the finest examples of Tudor architecture in the whole of the country.

Everything the Marquis owned was exceptional, even unique, and he was aware, now that Queen's Hoo was redecorated, renovated and refurbished, it would be the envy of all his friends, especially as it was situated so near to London.

Now his triumph at finding and displaying something exceptional was spoilt because Lottie had been struck down by a Spring Fever.

It flashed through his mind that rather than allow the whole thing to be ruined, he might call the party off and have it next week instead.

Then he knew that it was too late.

Although he was leaving earlier for the country than his friends, it would be impossible for him to notify them all and anyway it was unlikely that they would be at home.

They were probably already collecting their 'fair Cyprians' in various parts of London and he would be unable to contact them.

The Marquis was scowling as he drove on, vividly conscious of the empty seat in the phaeton beside him, where Lottie should have been sitting.

It took him, as he expected, six minutes under the hour to reach the gates of Queen's Hoo, which had been repainted and regilded, and their two lodges, which were also black and white like the house itself, had been done up and re-roofed.

He drove on, thinking that he had expected, when he reached here and Lottie had her first glimpse of the house at the end of the drive, to hear her exclamations of delight.

She was intelligent enough to realise that the Marquis not only, like all men, enjoyed being flattered, but was particularly pleased when his possessions were praised or he was complimented on something he had achieved.

There was no doubt that she would have clapped her pretty hands with delight and exclaimed over and over again at the magnificence of the black and white house to which they were drawing nearer and nearer.

The Marquis would have felt he deserved every word and every adjective, she expended over his cleverness at finding anything so lovely and unique.

He had to admit that it was a new possession he was proud to own and he was quite sure that his friends who had not yet seen Queen's Hoo would be awed into silence with their first glimpse of it.

The black beams had been repainted, the diamond panes of the windows had been replaced and now shone like jewels in the sunshine, while the eight gardeners Harry had engaged had achieved miracles in what had become a jungle.

It had been transformed into a vision of smooth green lawns, blossoming shrubs, mauve and white lilac with golden laburnum trees planted behind them, creating a Fairytale quality that was enchanting.

The Marquis drew up at the door at exactly the time Mr. Cunningham had notified Harry that he would arrive and, as the Marquis had expected, his manager was waiting for him at the top of the red carpet which covered the steps up to the newly painted front door.

Two grooms, who had been sitting behind the Marquis, hastily took the reins.

The new owner of Queen's Hoo stepped onto the red carpet to walk slowly and with dignity, but at the same time with an almost contemptuous air about him, to where Harry was standing.

"Good afternoon, my Lord!"

"Good afternoon, Dalton," the Marquis said. "Is everything ready for my guests, who should be arriving within the next hour?"

"I hope I have carried out all your instructions, my Lord," Harry said. "The pianos arrived yesterday."

"I should have thought that was running it rather fine," the Marquis remarked as if he was determined to find fault.

He walked into the hall, where the butler and four footmen were waiting.

As the Marquis had not seen them before, Harry said a little nervously,

"This is Jarvis, my Lord. He was with the Earl of Hull until he died."

The butler, a distinguished-looking man of middle- age, bowed politely.

The Marquis inclined his head and walked on into the drawing room, which he noticed was decorated in excellent taste with flowers, which scented the air.

He stood looking around him before he said,

"Arrange for gaming tables to be set up at the end of the room after dinner and be sure that there are enough new packs of cards, which were sent here last week."

"I received them, my Lord," Harry confirmed.

The Marquis walked down the passage and went into the library, which looked very different from how it had in the past.

The shelves lining the walls had all been filled with volumes bound in bright leather covers embossed with gold.

The curtains were of rich golden yellow brocade and the ceiling, which when he last saw it had been stained with damp and damaged in several places, was now restored to the architect's design for it when Queen's Hoo had first been built.

Harry had found the old drawings carefully preserved by his father in a sea chest that he had not noticed until they were moving what they wanted from Queen's Hoo into the Dower House.

When he realised what they were, he knew that the drawings were exactly what he needed to make what had been his home as perfect as he had always wanted to see it.

He had stood over the workmen, explaining, encouraging and inspiring them to create out of chaos what he thought of as perfection and he was sure that no one, not even the Marquis, could fail to be pleased with the result.

The Marquis, however, did not praise him, but merely said,

"I like this room and, as I doubt that any of my guests are ardent readers, I shall use it as my own."

The butler, who had followed them into the room at a respectful distance, obviously expecting to be taking orders, said,

"Mr. Dalton had the idea, my Lord, that that was what your Lordship would say, so I've put the grog tray in the corner. May I pour your Lordship a glass of champagne?"

"Thank you," the Marquis replied.

As Jarvis hurried to obey, Harry said,

"If your Lordship does not require me for the moment, there are a great many more things to see to in the Dining Hall."

"You have erected a stage as I told you?" the Marquis queried.

"Yes, indeed," Harry replied, "and I hope your Lordship will be pleased with the result."

"Then I will not detain you, Dalton."

With an effort Harry managed to bow politely before he left the room.

He went down the passage telling himself how much he disliked the Marquis. It would not have hurt him to say a few words of thanks for what he was well aware was a miracle of organisation.

'No one else could have done so much in so little time,' Harry fumed.

Then he laughed at himself because he wanted thanks for what, after all, was simply his job.

'If he gets as much pleasure out of it as I have,' he told himself, 'he will be lucky.'

He knew, if he was honest, that it had been an immense satisfaction to watch what had been his home being transformed from a wreck into the outstandingly beautiful building it was now.

'The trouble is,' he thought as he reached the Dining Hall, 'it is wasted on a man who has been spoilt by having too much of everything and a lot of illiterate doxies capable of appreciating only something sparkling that can be put round their necks!'

Then, as he entered the Dining Hall and saw that the flowers that the gardeners were bringing in to decorate it had been put in the wrong places, he was back doing what was expected of him, forgetting for the moment his own personal feelings in the matter.

*

Anthea had spent the afternoon practising on the spinet, which they had brought to the Dower House from Queen's Hoo.

It had belonged to her grandmother and was a very pretty piece of furniture, but rather difficult to play.

Anthea always dreamed that one day she would be able to afford a new piano such as she had read about and which she had always longed to feel under her fingers.

Mr. Meldosio had in his house a piano that was only ten years old, but he had described to her how different the very latest were and how much improvement had been made in the sound by the newest method of constructing the piano itself.

Mr. Meldosio had allowed Anthea to play his piano whenever she could spare the time and he also played to her and, although she was hardly aware of it, had taught her as if she was one of his pupils.

"I love coming here," she told him on her last visit a fortnight ago.

"And I love having you here, Miss Anthea," Mr. Meldosio replied. "It's a pity you were born a lady! For otherwise I feel sure you would have been acclaimed as a great concert pianist and people would have flocked to hear you."

Anthea laughed.

"You are flattering me and, although I enjoy hearing what you are saying, I know it's untrue. I shall never be able to play as well as you."

"That may be true technically," Mr. Meldosio agreed, "but you have something that cannot be taught and actually cannot be learnt."

"What is that," Anthea had asked.

"You play with your heart, Miss Anthea, and that is what really counts where music is concerned."

He paused before he went on,

"No, I think I am wrong. It's not your heart with which you play, but your soul, which is a very different thing and the divine touch is given only to angels."

"Now you are making me very conceited," Anthea laughed. "If I have a divine touch, as you call it, it is because you let me play on this lovely piano of yours and you have taught me so much about music that I feel I shall never have the chance to express all that you have given me."

Going away from Mr. Meldosio's house, Anthea thought over what he had said to her and told herself that he was exaggerating her talent because he was a foreigner.

At the same time she knew that music meant so much to her that it was impossible to think of her life without it.

She hummed melodies in her mind as she moved about the house and she could hear them on the wind when she was outside.

Often when she was riding alone in the Park, she thought that her horse's hoofs moving over the ground did so to a strange rhythm that was part of a song singing within her.

As she stood up from the spinet, she told herself that perhaps she would have been wise to go up to Mr. Meldosio's house to ask him if she could practise on his piano, but she felt that there was not really enough time.

He lived at the other end of the village and it would be a mistake for her to be tired before she performed tonight because she wanted to play her very best in order to help Harry.

Nanny was busy all the afternoon pressing the only decent gown that Anthea possessed.

Of white muslin, which Nanny had made for her a little while ago and which could certainly not be called a smart evening gown, it had a frill around the low neckline and the hem.

She wore it when she and Harry dined together at home and now Nanny had attempted to make it look a little more festive by adding a blue sash she had taken from one of her mother's gowns and which matched the blue of her eyes.

Nanny had at first been horrified at the idea of her going up to Queen's Hoo when the Marquis was there, but, when she knew that it was for Harry's benefit, she relented and agreed it was the only thing that could be done.

Nanny adored Harry as she had all his life.

She had come as a nurserymaid to Lady Colnbrooke just before Harry was born and five years later when Anthea arrived the old Nanny had retired and Nanny Ellen, as she was called, took over.

That was literally true, because as things grew more difficult after Lady Colnbrooke's death and Harry and Anthea's father began to realise how hard up they were, they had to manage with fewer and fewer servants.

It was Nanny who saw to everything and who made their lives very much more comfortable than they would have been without her.

Because she loved her 'two children' as she still called them, and they filled her whole life, Anthea knew that it would have been impossible for them to do without her or even to consider living anywhere unless she was there too.

But Harry was the one who really mattered and, although Nanny had been astonished by the transformation of Queen's Hoo and thought that 'her baby' was a genius for achieving so much, she still resented fiercely that he should have to pretend to be somebody other than he was.

As she complained often enough, he was nothing but a 'senior servant to his Lordship'.

"Do be careful what you say, Nanny," Anthea begged. "Harry would be furious if anyone at the Big House had any idea that he is really Lord Colnbrooke and I am sure if it became known that the Marquis would either sack him or he would have to resign."

"I'd not do anythin' that'd upset Master Harry," Nanny answered, "but it's a cryin' shame he should lose his home, the place where he should be livin' with his wife and children."

Anthea did not answer because there was nothing that she could say.

Now she went from the sitting room into the kitchen, and knew, as she saw Nanny concentrating on her gown that if it would help Harry, she would iron anything, even the carpets, if he asked her to do so.

Harry came back from the Big House later to change into his evening clothes and when he was dressed he said to Anthea,

"Now, you do understand, Anthea. You are to play in the Minstrels' Gallery until the dessert is put on the table. Then you slip down the staircase and start on the piano, which is at the side of the stage."

Anthea nodded and he went on,

"I have arranged a screen of flowers all around it so that you cannot be seen, but you will see the heads of the girls doing their *poses plastiques*, which will tell you when to start and to leave off. There is no need for you to try to look any closer."

He thought as he spoke of the poses that Anthea would not understand.

Nor would she have any idea that the poses were performed naked or with no more than a garland of flowers.

Anthea, however, had heard that the beautiful Lady Hamilton had delighted the King and Queen of Naples and, of course, Lord Nelson with her poses, many of which were Grecian.

She therefore reckoned that what the ballet dancers were doing tonight was very much the same and she told herself in that case they would want soft romantic music that would make them seem to those watching like young Goddesses straight from Mount Olympus.

"I understand exactly what you want, Harry," she said, "and don't worry about me."

"I do worry about you," he said, "but I know that there will be a great many things for me to see to in the stables with so many horses arriving and I am not yet absolutely convinced that the Head Groom is the right man for the post, but I could not get the man I wanted."

"It will be all right, I am sure it will," Anthea said soothingly. "The Marquis cannot expect everything to go like clockwork the very first time."

"But that is exactly what he does expect!" Harry said. "When he arrived he looked disagreeable, as if he was trying to find fault."

"Oh, no, how could he?" Anthea asked. "What did he say?"

"He did not say anything, it was just his general attitude," Harry replied.

Then, as if he thought that it was a mistake to talk about the Marquis to Anthea, he said,

"Anyway, do your best, old girl, and if the whole thing is a failure and I get the sack, I shall tell the Marquis exactly what I think of him, which would give me a great deal of pleasure!"

"Oh, no, Harry, *no!*" Anthea begged. "Please be conciliatory and don't upset him unnecessarily. You know you would hate it if you could no longer manage Queen's Hoo and the estate and there was somebody else doing it in your place."

She knew as she spoke that she had said the right thing for Harry smiled and said,

"You are quite right, Anthea, and I am jolly lucky to have what I do have. If it means I must kowtow to a man who thinks he is Lord of the Universe, then I will do it!"

He turned towards the door before he added,

"Oh, by the way, don't forget to warn Nanny not to say a word to the servants that might make them curious as to who you are."

"Nanny knows that already," Anthea answered. "Go away and do what you have to do and stop worrying about us."

Soon after Harry had left she and Nanny set out to walk through the Park to Queen's Hoo.

The Dower House was at the very Southern end of the Park and there was a beautiful walk through the woods, which saved them from having to go on the gravelly drive.

The sunset had turned the beech trees to silver and the beauty of the sky seemed to bring a special melody into Anthea's mind.

They walked slowly, for Nanny could not hurry, and when they reached Queen's Hoo they went in through the kitchen entrance. From the noise and the chatter the place seemed a hive of activity and very different from when they had been living there.

Nobody took any notice of them as they hurried down the flagged passage and up the back staircase, which took them to the housekeeper's room on the first floor.

Harry had transformed this too as he had transformed everything else in the house.

Now the walls were patterned with a pretty paper, there was a new sofa and comfortable chairs, besides a round table at which the housekeeper could eat with the butler, the two head-housemaids and, if there were any in the house, a lady's maid.

Mrs. Andrews, a homely woman whom Harry had engaged because she was so experienced, greeted them with pleasure.

"Mr. Dalton said you'd be comin'," she said to Anthea, "and I'm sorry to hear about your poor father havin' a bad hand."

"It's unfortunate, is it not?" Anthea agreed.

"But I'm sure you'll play very nicely, my dear," Mrs. Andrews said, "and if you'd like to go down to the Minstrels' Gallery, as I understand you know the way, I'll look after your friend until you are ready to go home."

"Thank you very much," Anthea smiled.

She laid her long velvet evening cape, which had been her mother's and which she had worn to walk through the woods, over a chair and stood for a moment tidying herself in front of the mirror that hung on the wall.

Her dress looked very pretty, she thought and, as she had no jewellery, Nanny had tied around her long neck a piece of blue velvet that matched her sash and attached to it a little locket that had belonged to her mother.

It gave her, Anthea thought, a finishing touch and, as she smoothed her hair, she thought she appeared quiet and unobtrusive, and certainly no one would look at her when there were ballet dancers about.

Leaving the housekeeper's room, she walked down the stairs, which came out by the pantry, and on the other side of the passage was the Dining Hall.

Here there was a small door, hardly noticeable, which opened onto a short staircase leading up to the Minstrels' Gallery.

It had been a vantage point for Anthea when she was a child from which to watch the parties that took place in her mother's time.

She was not supposed to do so, but she had found it irresistible not to slip down from the night nursery with bare feet and in her nightgown and climb the stairs to the Minstrels' Gallery to peep through the screen carved with ivy leaves.

This was the screen that prevented those below from seeing the musicians themselves, while hearing their music.

Now, as she reached the Gallery, her heart gave a leap of excitement, for there was the piano that Harry had told her was arriving.

It was, in fact, the very latest and most up-to-date model, just as Mr. Meldosio had described to her.

It was one thing to hear a description, but quite another to see and touch it.

Then Anthea realised that it was so much bigger, more impressive and certainly far more exciting than she had ever envisaged it would be.

She touched the ivory keys with her fingers as if she caressed them and then, because she was curious, she moved to the front of the Gallery to look down onto the Dining Hall.

It was far lovelier than she remembered, for not only had Harry covered the walls with a very beautiful deep red paper but there were also pictures that Anthea had never seen before.

She was sure that there was a Rubens over the marble mantelpiece, which had been added during the last century and she guessed that a picture on another wall that she could not see very clearly was a Rembrandt.

There was also a Van Dyke, doubtless of one of the Marquis's ancestors, which had been placed behind his chair at the top of the table.

The table itself was as she had always longed to see it.

There was no tablecloth, following the fashion brought in by the Prince Regent and the polished wood seemed to shine as brightly as the gold and silver ornaments that decorated it.

The gold candelabra, which each held six candles, ran the length of the table and in the centre there was a magnificent model of a ship in full sail, which Anthea longed to see more closely.

Harry had been sparing with the flower decorations, which, as they were orchids, Anthea knew had come down from London.

There was a cluster of crystal glasses at every diner's place and also the back of each chair was decorated by a silver plate bearing the Marquis's crest.

Then to her surprise she realised that the servants were removing one place from the table. Instead of twenty-four, as Harry had said there would be, there were now only twenty-three places.

She wondered who the missing person was, whether it was a man or a woman.

'The Marquis will not be pleased at his plans being changed,' she thought to herself.

Then, moving away from the front of the Gallery, she sat down at the piano.

As she started to play, the exquisite sounds that came from her fingers made her forget everything, even the Marquis!

She was lost in a Fairytale world that, as far as she was concerned, could be told only in the music that came from her heart.

chapter three

It was a good thing that Harry had the forethought to tell one of the servants to remind Anthea to go down to the stage when the dessert was being put on the table.

She was so far away in her dreams, finding the music she could make on this piano so different from anything that had been possible for her before, that she had forgotten everything but the enchanting new horizons opening in front of her.

She started when she realised that a footman in the Marquis's livery was standing beside her and, as she looked up at him, he whispered,

"We are serving dessert now, miss."

It seemed incredible that she had actually forgotten what was happening down below at the Marquis's party.

Now, as she took her fingers from the keys and could hear the laughter and raised voices, she smiled and nodded to the footman to show that she understood.

He tiptoed away from the Minstrels' Gallery and Anthea rose from the piano stool.

Because she was curious she went to the carved screen that ran the length of one wall and peeped through it.

Now, with the candles alight in the candelabra on the table and the guests seated around it, she thought that nothing could look more attractive or more like a picture from one of her father's books.

Then, as she looked at the head of the table and saw the Marquis, she realised that he looked exactly as she had expected.

He was sitting upright in a high-backed carved armchair that was like a throne, watching his guests laughing and chattering around him with an air of detached cynicism that was almost contemptuous.

Never had Anthea imagined that a man could look so magnificent or so omnipotent in his own way and yet have a cynical twist to his lips as if nothing around him were really to his satisfaction.

At the same time she realised that he was different, not only from his guests but from any man she had ever seen.

She stared at him, feeling because he was so different it was hard to look at anyone else.

Then, remembering that she must go to the platform, she had a quick glance at the ladies around the table and thought with a sense of shock that their gowns were indecently low.

She had never imagined any lady would wear anything so immodest in the company of gentlemen.

As she turned away, recalling her instructions, she told herself that it was because she was seeing the lady guests from a different angle from those seated at the table.

She was above them looking down, while the gentlemen were sitting beside them.

Even so, she knew that her mother would certainly have disapproved of their appearance and she suspected too that because they were actresses they would be painted and powdered even though they were not on the stage.

'I must not be critical,' Anthea told herself as she climbed down the narrow oak staircase to the floor below, 'and if I am, I must certainly not tell Harry, since he told me to concentrate only on my playing and not pry on the Marquis and his friends.'

But when she found, to her delight, another piano identical to the one in the Gallery and sat down on the stool in front of it, she was thinking of the Marquis.

Although she had seen him only from a distance, she knew now that his name was appropriate.

It was Charlie who had said laughingly,

"He looks like an eagle, which is his nickname, and he behaves like one. After all, the eagle is the King of the Birds."

"How can he be called 'Eagle' when it is part of his title?" Anthea enquired curiously.

"The story goes and, of course, there are innumerable stories about him," Charlie replied, "that when he was born he had an unusual amount of very dark hair and somebody said to his father,

"'He looks like a small eagle!'"

"The Marquis of Eaglescliffe laughed and said,

'Well that is appropriate anyway.'

"From that time on he always called his son 'Eagle' rather than by any of the names he was christened with."

"And you say he acts like one?" Anthea questioned.

"A very fierce, very aggressive and very dangerous eagle," Charlie had said jokingly.

Later Anthea had learned from Harry that the nickname had caught the fancy of the public.

When the Marquis's horses romped home to victory on the Racecourses, as they invariably did, the crowd would chant, 'Eagle! Eagle!' and those who had won money through backing the favourite would applaud.

'He is indeed like an eagle,' Anthea said to herself as she ran her fingers over the keyboard. 'I wish I could see him a little closer.'

Then she remembered how angry Harry would be at the idea and concentrated on playing the soft romantic music that she thought would be correct for the girls who were to perform on the stage.

As Harry had told her, she was boxed in so that it was impossible see anything but the stage straight ahead of her.

Then, because the piano was open, she could just catch a glimpse of the girls' heads when they came on.

The first one received a burst of applause and, although Anthea could see her hands raised above her head and was aware that she was standing very still, she was unable to see more. She knew only when the clapping started again that she had finished her turn.

Another girl took her place and obviously her performance was very much appreciated, because there were not only claps, but shouts of 'bravo!' from the men seated round the dining room table.

Anthea wondered if the Marquis was applauding and felt perceptively that he was just watching, probably disdainfully and would not exert himself or show his appreciation even if he thought that the performance was a good one.

'Poor Harry,' Anthea thought. 'It's unfair that he should have to work for somebody who is so difficult. Any other man would have been enthusiastic over what has been done at Queen's Hoo.'

She told herself, as she had done before, that she hated the Marquis. And yet in a way that was not quite true.

Because he had spent so much money on the house, the farms and anything that Harry had suggested on the estate, she could not help feeling, because it meant so much to them both, that she should be grateful to him.

They were also free of debts that she knew would have crippled Harry for life and humiliated him because there had been very little he could have done about them.

'At least the Marquis has saved us from worrying and enabled us to do up the Dower House and we can now afford more comforts and better food than we have had for years,' Anthea admitted to herself.

Even though she told herself this about the Marquis, she still felt herself shiver at the thought of him.

A third girl had come onto the stage and now there was a sound that was like a gasp of surprise.

Then there was laughter as well as applause and although florid remarks were shouted from the table, either Anthea could not hear them or else they made no sense to her.

The third girl finished her pose and then all three appeared together.

This time, because Anthea could see their heads close together as they posed in a group, she longed to know exactly what they were doing.

The noise of the applause was now tumultuous and again there were shouts and cheers and then finally loud prolonged applause as they left the stage.

Anthea continued to play, until there were sounds that told her that the ladies were now leaving the dining room. This meant that the gentlemen would move up the table to be nearer to the Marquis and would drink the port and brandy that was taken round by the servants.

She had seen this happening from the Minstrels' Gallery when she was a child at the dinner parties arranged by her father and mother in the Dining Hall.

Then after her mother's death her father had once or twice entertained his friends, although it had been a tremendous effort to provide the sort of dinner that he required for them.

By this time they were growing short of servants and it was only because Anthea helped Nanny, who was in her turn helping the cook in the kitchen, that they managed it.

Because of this Anthea knew how things should be done in what Nanny would have called 'a gentleman's house' and she knew that once the gentlemen were left behind in the dining room they would start talking.

That would be her opportunity to slip away as Harry had told her to do.

She, however, played for another five minutes, thinking it would seem too abrupt to stop the music just because the ladies had left the room.

Then, as reluctantly she brought to an end the melody she was playing, she stood for a moment looking at the piano, thinking that she would give everything she possessed to own anything so marvellous.

It was then that a footman came to her side and she looked at him in surprise, wondering what he could want.

"His Lordship says, miss, that he wishes you now to play in the drawing room."

Anthea's eyes widened and for a moment she could only stammer,

"I – in the – drawing room?"

"Yes, miss. I'll show you the way."

"No, no, of course not," Anthea said desperately. "Please – would you be obliging enough to tell his Lordship that when you brought me the message I had already left?"

"But that would not be true, would it?" a voice asked from behind her.

She started as she realised that the Marquis had come onto the stage without her being aware of it.

Now, standing beside the piano, he seemed, as he towered above her, enormous and she thought too that his nickname was indeed apt.

Never could she imagine a man's hair could be so black, as were his eyes. His nose was aquiline and yet, although he looked like an eagle, he was in his own way extremely handsome.

The footman disappeared and Anthea stood facing the Marquis for a moment finding it hard to think clearly.

He was looking at her in a penetrating manner that might have made her feel even more shy had she not realised that he was expecting to find that the pianist was Mr. Meldosio.

"I understood," he said slowly looking at her, she thought, from the top of her head down to her toes, "that a man called 'Meldosio' was playing for me this evening."

With difficulty Anthea found her voice.

"That – that was what was – arranged – my Lord," she managed to say, "b-but his hand was – damaged in an – accident and I took his – place."

"Who are you? What is your name?"

"A-Anthea – Meldosio."

There was a distinct pause before Anthea could remember that she was supposed to be Mr. Meldosio's daughter.

She knew, because she was frightened by the Marquis being so overwhelming, that in a way he seemed to menace her.

"Then I must congratulate you on the music, Miss Meldosio," he said. "I did not expect a woman to play with such feeling."

"I-I am – glad you are – pleased, my Lord," Anthea said hesitatingly. "But I am afraid now – I have to – return home."

"That is something I have no wish for you to do," the Marquis replied. "In fact I feel that the music you have played has been a major contribution to the success of my party. You will therefore continue to play in the drawing room."

"N-no – I am sorry – I-I – "

As Anthea stopped, she looked up into the Marquis's eyes and the words died away on her lips.

It flashed through her mind that, if she refused, Harry might suffer.

Harry would be called to task because she would not obey the Marquis, who, as she had been told over and over again, always had his own way on everything.

She did not speak but only stood looking at him and, as if he compelled her to do what he wanted, she said in a childlike voice,

"M-must I – play in the – drawing room?"

"I insist," the Marquis said firmly. "And if, as I imagine, you do not wish to be noticed, I suggest that you go there quickly while the ladies are upstairs and the gentlemen are still here."

Anthea drew in her breath, but, because there seemed to be nothing more she could say, she picked up her handkerchief from where she had laid it on the side of the piano and, without looking at the Marquis, left the stage by the small door that she had used to climb up to the Minstrels' Gallery.

Then because she was frightened, frightened of the Marquis and frightened too of how angry Harry would be when he knew, she ran as quickly as she could down the long corridor that led to the hall and to the drawing room, which opened out of it.

As she entered the room, it was empty except for two footmen arranging gaming tables at the far end and she saw that the piano had been placed in an alcove in front of one of the bow windows that looked out onto the Rose Garden.

It had been set sideways and quickly, because she was so afraid of being seen, she said to the footmen,

"Will you please move the piano for me? His Lordship wishes me to play and I would like it to be straight."

"Of course, miss," one of the footmen replied.

He moved the piano as she requested, raising the lid for her, so that she felt that it was also a protection.

Then she had another idea.

She had noticed that the profusion of flowers with which the room was decorated and had seen that two huge Chinese vases on ebony stands which were filled with white lilac had been placed on either side of the fireplace.

She was sure that the vases were really too valuable to be used for flowers, but that was not her problem.

She asked the footmen to set them on each side of the piano, making a screen for her when she sat down to play.

They had only just carried out her instructions when the door of the drawing room opened and the ladies, who had been upstairs, came into the room.

Anthea therefore began to play very softly, hoping that they would not be aware of her presence.

She could hear their voices and she thought to her surprise how uneducated they were and what her mother would have termed 'common'.

Then she heard one woman say,

"He says to me, 'Dolly, how can I charm you away from Shelgrave. I'll promise you better horses and a smarter carriage than he's given you'."

"What did you answer?" another woman enquired.

"I says to him, 'what do you suggest, my Lord?' and he answers, 'What about a bracelet for a pretty wrist?'

"I give him a sharp look and says,

"'Depends what it's made of, doesn't it?'"

The other woman laughed.

"That was quick of you, Dolly!"

"That's what I thought, and when he says, 'what about diamonds? Would that please you?'

"'Give me a necklace to go with it,' I says, 'and I'm yours!'"

There was a peal of laughter and Anthea thought it a very strange conversation for two women to have.

She wondered if what the Peer in question had been offering Dolly was, in point of fact, a strange proposal of marriage.

Then she was sure that Noblemen did not marry actresses and the whole conversation seemed very mysterious.

'I suppose, like the Marquis,' she thought, 'the gentleman in question is very very rich.'

There was one thing she felt quite certain about, that Harry would never be able to offer an actress a diamond necklace or for that matter, horses and a carriage.

Although thanks to the sale of Queen's Hoo, they were very much better off than they had been before, they could not 'throw money about' as Nanny had said, 'seeing it would not last for ever'.

Almost as if she was his mother rather than his sister, Anthea worried in case Harry would get extravagant ideas through working for the Marquis.

It had been fascinating for him to be able to spend as much as he wanted in doing up the house, building onto the stables, repairing the cottages in the village and replacing everything that had fallen to bits on the farms.

At the same time she was aware that the renovation of the Dower House, for which Harry had paid, had come to quite a considerable sum.

'We must be very very careful,' Anthea thought.

She wondered how much the Marquis's party had cost in food, drink and flowers, as she knew much of it had come down from London besides the three pianos.

She was wondering if ever again she would have the chance of playing on the new pianos and if she might perhaps creep into Queen's Hoo when the

Marquis was not in residence to play in the Minstrels' Gallery.

Then, as she thought despondently that it was very unlikely she would ever be able to do such a thing, she heard the deep voices of the men as they came into the drawing room.

She also caught a glimpse of them under the raised lid of the piano as they moved across the room to where the women were sitting.

Then she saw that they had all moved to the gaming tables and soon there were shrieks of delight as one of the women won and, while she went on playing, she thought how ignorant she was of gaming.

She knew that it was part of life in London, not only for the bucks and beaux in the Clubs, where they played for very high stakes but also in the houses of the great hostesses, who themselves were often inveterate gamblers.

'That is one thing I shall never do,' Anthea reflected.

Then she told herself she had many compensations that they would not understand and she played for them in sound, what the woods meant to her, the flowers, the birds that woke her in the mornings, singing outside her bedroom window and were an irrepressible joy.

She played for them the stories she told herself, which had become so much part of her existence that she believed in them as if what happened in them were real.

Then she expressed in what she was playing what she felt when she rode early in the morning when the dew was still on the grass.

The melody she had heard in the rustle of the trees overhead was in the notes she played.

There was the first star coming out in a translucent sky as the sun slipped away behind the oaks in the park, there was the high shrill squeak of a bat, then the song of the nightingales as they moved from tree to tree.

The music seemed to flow from her fingers and every note was a new image of what she had heard and seen.

Suddenly she opened her eyes and with a start realised that the Marquis was leaning on the piano beside her.

Because she had forgotten his very existence, for a moment she could only stare at him and feel as if she came back through clouds of dreams to reality.

Then as her fingers fell from the keys onto her lap he said in a deep voice,

"Who taught you to play like that?"

"I-I think – really – I taught myself."

"And what you played is your own composition?"

She smiled as if he had asked a rather foolish question and she replied,

"They are the sounds I listen to when I am riding in the woods or I hear in the darkness of the night – in fact always when I am – alone."

"That is what I thought," he said.

Because she was surprised at the way he answered her, without really thinking Anthea rose to her feet and as she did so she saw that the drawing room was empty.   There was no one there except for the Marquis.

"Everyone has gone to bed," he told her.

"Then – I can – go home?"

"First I have something to show you," the Marquis replied. "Come with me."

He put out his hand and taking her wrist drew her from behind the piano.

For the first time she was able to look at the drawing room and she wanted to see the new pictures on the walls and the effect of the gold leaf where it topped the cornice and the ceiling, which had been skilfully restored.

This had been achieved after Harry, with the greatest difficulty, had managed to find craftsmen expert in plasterwork.

But, as the Marquis drew her from the room, she was conscious that he was giving her an order and it was impossible for her to defy it against his wishes.

They crossed the hall and went up the staircase that she had loved as a child and which she saw had now been polished until the old oak of which it was carved shone with a brilliance it had never possessed before.

Now they were on the first floor, moving past the State bedrooms she had known so well, but which now had been transformed out of all recognition so that they were worthy of the Kings and Queens after whom they had been named.

Still the Marquis walked on and she wondered as he went a little farther down the corridor what he wished to show her, and hoped that he would not be too long about it, as Nanny was waiting to take her home.

He opened a door and she realised that he was taking her into what had been her father's room. She knew that Harry had taken special care to make it as magnificent as it must have been when Queen's Hoo was first built.

There was one candelabrum with three candles alight by the huge carved oak bed, which even though he hated doing so, Harry had sold to the Marquis with the other State beds, because they were too large to be moved and anyway they had nowhere to put them.

The Master bed was the most heavily carved and undoubtedly the biggest in the whole house.

It had formerly looked sad and shabby with its silk curtains faded and worn, but now Anthea, glancing at it, realised that it was now, in its way, as magnificent as the Marquis.

Harry had draped the bed with crimson curtains of the most expensive velvet he could obtain, the curtains that covered the windows were of the same velvet and on the floor was a thick Persian carpet that echoed the same colour.

There were new pictures, furniture that belonged to the Marquis and, as Anthea had never seen before in the room, huge vases of lilies.

In the light of the candles it all looked so attractive that she just stood staring at the transformation of the room she had known since she was a child.

Then, as she knew that the Marquis was waiting for her to say something appreciative, she stammered,

"It is – magnificent and – very – very beautiful!"

"As you are," he said.

She was so surprised at the compliment that she turned to look at him and, when she did so, to her astonishment, his arms went round her.

"You are not only beautiful," the Marquis said, "but your music is enthralling and entrances me."

Because she thought that what was happening could not be true, Anthea could only stare at him.

"Why should we try to put into words what we both feel when there is a so much easier way to express it?"

As he spoke, his lips came down on Anthea's and held hers captive.

She could not believe that she was not dreaming.

As she felt the Marquis's lips, hard and possessive, it flashed through her mind that this was not what she had expected a kiss would be.

At the same time he should not be kissing her and she must stop him from doing so.

But he had enveloped her so that her arms were imprisoned and she could not move any more than she could take her mouth away from his.

At first she was too surprised even to think.

Then, as she attempted to struggle he prevented her, until feeling utterly and completely helpless she thought that she must faint with the shock of what was happening.

She was astonished by the strength of the Marquis and, as he was so overpowering, she felt that she had lost her identity and was no longer herself.

She would feel his lips become more demanding, more possessive, and she had the strange idea, although it seemed impossible, that he was excited by her.

And yet she could still not really appreciate that she was being kissed by a man whom she had never seen before although inevitably she had thought of him every day for months.

Then, as the Marquis twisted her lips a little, she felt a very strange and frightening sensation almost like a flash of lightning seep through her.

But she managed to free one of her hands and attempt to push him away from her.

As she did so, she felt his hand cover her breast and with a streak of fear that overcame everything she fought to free her lips from his.

"No – *no!*" she managed to gasp and her voice sounded very unlike her own and almost inarticulate.

"No – please – you must not – kiss me!"

"I *have* kissed you," the Marquis said in his deep voice, "and I found it so delightful that I intend to kiss you again."

Desperately Anthea turned her head away from him, saying,

"No! No – you must – not do so!"

"Why not?" he asked. "You are adorable, Anthea. We will talk about it in the morning, but I promise you anything you want of me, so long as you will play to me your music, which is an unexpected delight, and let me teach you about love, of which I suspect you know very little."

He pulled her even closer against him and then because she was frightened, she sent a prayer to her mother,

'Help me – Mama. Help – me! What – am I to do?'

Then it was as if her mother was there beside her and guiding her and she knew the answer.

For a moment she ceased to struggle and merely said in a voice that was hardly audible,

"Please may I have a – drink? I am – very thirsty."

The Marquis gave a little laugh of sheer amusement.

"Of course," he said. "You have been playing for a long time and it was very remiss of me not to send you refreshments, which I should have done."

He took his arms from her as he spoke and walked across the room to where, as Anthea knew, there was a communicating door into what had been her mother's boudoir.

As the Marquis passed into the boudoir, Anthea ran to the mantelpiece and felt with fingers that trembled the panelling on the right side of it.

For a moment she could not find the catch that opened the door to one of the secret passages where she and Harry had played as children.

Then, as she heard the clink of a glass from the room next door, the panel swung open and she slipped through it being careful to close it behind her very gently so that there was no sound.

A split second later she heard the Marquis come back into the bedroom with what she imagined was a glass of champagne in his hand.

He stood still and she knew that he was looking for her.

Then he called out,

"Are you hiding from me, Anthea? If so, I shall find you. I promise I will not allow you to escape me!"

Anthea stood very still, listening.

She knew only too well that the flooring of this part of the secret passage was rough with age and, if she moved, it would not be difficult for the Marquis to hear where she was and he might be astute enough to find the hidden catch.

She heard him walk to the window and pull back the curtains and then he opened the door of the bathroom that had previously been a powder closet.

As she knew, there was nowhere anybody could hide in there.

Then he crossed to the other side of the bed, where there was the door into the passage and, as she heard him turn the handle, she knew, although she had not been aware of it at the time, that he had locked the door when he had brought her into his bedroom.

She felt her heart beating indignantly at the thought that he had done such a thing, but she did not move, only held her breath.

Once again the Marquis looked behind the curtains.

Then she thought that he had tugged at the bell-pull beside the bed and was standing waiting so that it was still impossible for her to move away.

A minute or so later, as if he had been listening for the Marquis's call, the servant knocked on the door that led into the passage and the Marquis turned the key in the lock.

"Ready for bed, my Lord?" a voice asked cheerily.

"Is there any other way into this room, Haynes, except through this door?" the Marquis asked.

"No, my Lord. Why should there be, unless, of course, one goes through the sitting room."

"That is what I thought," the Marquis replied.

He did not say anything more, but Anthea, listening, was certain that he was beginning to undress.

She thought he would go to the bathroom to wash and then she would be able to move away.

But, when he did so, she could still hear Haynes, his valet, moving about the room.

'I must wait,' she told herself, even though she was impatient to be gone.

It was dark and stuffy in the secret passage, but she knew every inch of it and was not afraid, except that she might be heard and the Marquis by some uncanny means of his own would be able to follow her.

Finally, after what seemed a long time, she heard Haynes walk across the room and suspected that he blew out the candles by the bed before he said,

"Good night, my Lord. I'll call your Lordship as usual at eight o'clock."

"Good night, Haynes."

It was obvious from the sound of his voice that the Marquis was now in bed.

Still Anthea waited.

Only when she was sure that he was either asleep or at least not listening for any particular noise did she take off her slippers and move very cautiously, step by step, away from the door in the panelling.

The secret passage ran across the front of the house and was tricky to negotiate at night because to pass each window one had to go down several small steps and bend one's head before one climbed up other steps and back into the passage.

It presented very little difficulty however to Anthea, who felt the way with her hands and she knew that she could at any time, if it was safe, come out in one of the State bedrooms.

This particular passage, her father always thought, had been built later than the house and was the work of the Jesuits during the reign of Queen Elizabeth, when they found shelter with the Lord Colnbrooke of the day and from Queen's Hoo had been able to escape across the Channel to freedom.

Anthea was, however, at this moment not concerned with the history of the house, but in making sure that she did not burst into a bedroom that was occupied.

Then, as she was passing the Charles II Room, she heard a woman's voice shrill and common, exclaim,

"You intend to kill him!"

"Of course I do," a man's voice answered. "You know damned well that if he is not dead by Wednesday, I shall lose a packet. In fact, if I am not careful, I shall find myself being taken to the Debtors' Prison."

"How could you have been so stupid as to get into such a position?" the woman asked.

"It's no use going over that now," the man replied. "What I want you to do, Milly, is to go along to his room and tell him that you could not bear to think of him alone when everybody else was having so much fun. Tell him I am drunk and no use to you and then make sure he understands what is expected of him."

He gave a rather unpleasant laugh as he added,

"That should not be difficult where Eaglescliffe is concerned!"

"Suppose he isn't interested in me?"

"You make sure he is! Then when he is asleep you kill him."

"How do you expect me to do that? With my fingernails?"

"Don't be facetious, Milly! This is serious! I have over there in the dressing table a long thin stiletto. It came from Italy and is the finest thing you have ever seen. Stick it in the right place in a man's heart and he dies instantly! If you do it properly, it leaves only a tiny mark."

"You're askin' a great deal," Milly replied sullenly.

"Now, listen, sweetie, you know what it means to me! If my horse wins the Derby, which it will with Eaglescliffe's out of the way, you and I will be flying high. I swear you will never regret helping me."

"I'm a fool, but I suppose that's what I've got to do," Milly said.

"How can you refuse me when you know what we mean to each other?"

"All right! All right! But I'd sooner not do this. Suppose I'm caught?"

"No one will suspect you. He will not be found until the morning and, as I say, it's unlikely anyone will think it is foul play if you bring the stiletto back with you. In any case we shall both have a perfect alibi being here together."

"I suppose it's all right," Milly sighed, "but I don't like it!"

"Nor do I, but there is nothing else I can do except to put a bullet through my head."

"No, no!" Milly exclaimed. "How can I lose you?"

"Then get on with it," the man said, "and hurry back to me as quickly as you can! I'd be jealous if it was not something that had to be done!"

"There's no need for you to feel jealous of any other man," Milly murmured. "It's only, I'm frightened of what you're askin' me to do."

"I swear there will be no difficulties. Wrap the stiletto up in your handkerchief and put it in your dressing gown pocket. Take it off as you get into bed beside him and then wait until he falls asleep before you use it."

The man gave a chuckle before he said,

"No one knows better than you, Milly, how to tire a man out."

"All right," Milly said, "you win! Give me a kiss before I go."

It was then that Anthea realised with horror what she had been overhearing.

How was it possible? How could anyone plan to kill the Marquis in such a dastardly manner?

She was horrified, but her first thought was that it was none of her business and the sooner she was away from Queen's Hoo the better.

Then she knew that she could not let it happen.

Whatever she might feel about the Marquis, however he had behaved towards her, and she did not want to think about that for the moment, she could not let him be murdered in such horrifying and disgusting manner.

It was something that she was certain her father would have deprecated and, if the Marquis died, then somebody else, even worse, might take over Queen's Hoo.

Then the thought of her mother was like a trumpet call in her ears.

It was not only the Marquis she had to save but Harry and his job, and the people, their people, whom they had been able to help and who might in other hands be neglected.

Anthea put on the slippers she was carrying and started to run back along the passage, down the little steps beneath each window, up the other side and on, not worrying now if anyone could hear her.

She was intent only on reaching the Marquis before Milly was there and ready to kill him.

She was breathless by the time she reached the door in the panelling she had escaped through only twenty minutes earlier, thinking that her troubles were over.

Now, with her heart beating and her hands trembling, she reached out for the catch and opened it.

As the door in the panelling slid sideways, she saw, as she expected, that the room was in darkness except for the light coming from the uncurtained window.

Anthea drew in a deep breath and then she said,

"My Lord! Wake up, my Lord!"

Because, she thought later, the Marquis had been a soldier, he woke instantly.

She heard him move his head and, as she did so, she said,

"Listen to me! This is important – !"

"Where are you? What has happened?" the Marquis interrupted.

"There is no time to talk about it," Anthea said. "A woman is coming to your bedroom. She is on her way now. She intends, after you have been – together, to kill you. She has a stiletto ready to do so. Lock your door and whatever you do – don't let her in."

"What on earth are you saying? What is happening?" the Marquis asked.

Anthea knew that however puzzled he might be, he was fully awake and had understood what she was saying.

She therefore stepped back into the passage, shut the door in the panelling and retracing her steps, picked up her slippers from where she had left them and hurried on, past the Charles II room, letting herself out into a boudoir two rooms beyond it.

She did not ask herself now if there was anybody sleeping in the bedrooms because, with any luck, they would not hear her.

She was sure that the boudoir, at any rate, would be empty and, as she opened a panel in the wall, she knew by the darkness inside it that her assumption had been right.

She groped her way to the door leading to the passage, where she could see her way clearly.

Although some of the candles in the elaborate silver sconces, which bore the Marquis's crest, had been extinguished by the night-footman, it was easy to find her way to the end of the first floor, through the baize door that led into the servants' quarters and to the housekeeper's room.

She opened the door to find that Nanny was alone there and asleep in an armchair in front of the fireplace.

She looked very peaceful, but she gave a little cry as Anthea touched her shoulder and she sat up abruptly.

"Where have you been, I'd like to know?" she asked. "I expected you back hours ago!"

"I know, Nanny, and I will tell you about it as we go home," Anthea replied.

She picked up her cloak from where she had left it over the chair and slipped it over her shoulders.

Nanny put on her bonnet and the black shawl she wore over her grey dress.

Then they were hurrying down a side staircase that led to one of the doors into the garden.

"Why are we goin' out this way?" Nanny enquired.

"I think it is best in case any of the kitchen staff are awake that they don't see us," Anthea replied.

Nanny obviously saw the logic of this, but she said nothing.

Only when they were walking briskly down the drive, the starlight guiding their way, did she ask,

"What made you so late? Master Harry would not like you hangin' about when you should have come home."

"It's not my fault," Anthea replied.

"Well, I expect you've got some good excuse," Nanny said, "but I hope you've not been mixin' with that Marquis and his raffish friends. I don't know what you father would say at such goings on. Queen's Hoo has never seen anythin' like it and the sooner they all goes back to London the better!"

"I agree with you, Nanny," Anthea said, "but I am very tired."

She did not say any more until they reached the Dower House.

Then Anthea remembered with a sinking of her heart that Harry would be waiting for her.

Harry would certainly want a much fuller explanation of what had happened when she should have been ready to go home.

They went in by the kitchen door because Nanny had the key and, while she set about making a cup of tea, Anthea went through into the small hall, feeling sure that Harry would not have gone to bed if she was not back.

She went into the study, where they sat when they were alone and did not use the drawing room.

As she expected, she found him there.

He was lying on the leather sofa, his head on a cushion and he was fast asleep.

She saw that he had taken off his coat and shoes and she knew by the way he was breathing that he was exhausted, both from all that he had had to do and because he had been so tense and nervous that things might not go right.

She wondered what he would say if she told him what had happened tonight and then told herself that he must never know.

Slowly and gently so as not to wake him, she took off her velvet evening cloak and put it over him in case he should feel cold.

Then she blew out the candles, which were guttering low on the desk and, slipping out of the study, closed the door very softly behind her.

She went back into the kitchen and told Nanny that Harry was asleep and it would be a great mistake to wake him.

"He's tired out, that he is!" Nanny said.

Anthea hesitated.

"As he has so much on his mind, Nanny, I think it would be a mistake for him to know how late we arrived home. It would only upset him."

For a moment she thought that Nanny was going to argue with her and she said hastily,

"I will talk to you about it in the morning, but don't say anything to Harry."

"I don't know what the world's comin' to, that I don't!" Nanny said. "Now, hurry off to bed, Miss Anthea, and I'll bring you up a glass of hot milk."

Anthea knew that she had won and Nanny would not say anything to Harry.

Only as she climbed into bed to wait for her milk did she find herself worrying over the Marquis.

Had he understood what she had said? Had he locked his door?

If not, in the morning they would find him dead and she would be the only person who knew who had killed him.

CHAPTER FOUR

Anthea was awoken by Nanny pulling back the curtains in her bedroom.

"It's ten o'clock, dear," she said, "and I think you should get up or you'll be late for Church."

"Ten o'clock!" Anthea exclaimed. "How can it be so late?"

She sat up in bed, thinking as she did so that she had been dreaming a wonderful dream in which everything had seemed beautiful and happy.

Now she remembered what had happened last night and with a little tremor in her voice she asked,

"Is everything – all right? What has – happened at the – Big House?"

"What should happen?" Nanny asked tartly. "Except that those houris from London are sleepin' a great deal later than you are."

Anthea did not reply.

She only said after a moment,

"And Harry is all right?"

"He slept like a log all night, accordin' to him," Nanny replied. "Then after breakfast he rushed off to work his fingers to the bone and not a word of thanks, you can be sure of that!"

"You did not tell him we were – late?" Anthea persisted.

"He didn't ask and them as asks no questions gets told no lies."

Nanny walked towards the door, adding as she did,

"I'll have your breakfast ready by the time you come down."

Relieved that at least Harry did not realise how late she had been and, knowing in that case she would have to make no explanation, Anthea washed in the new bathroom in cold water.

She then put on the gown that Nanny had left out for her on a chair.

It was a new one and she knew that she would not have been allowed to go out in it except on a Sunday.

It was very simple because Nanny could not make anything elaborate, but the material was of sprigged muslin, which was more expensive than anything they had been able to afford in the past.

Anthea knew that Nanny had ordered it specially from the carrier who never had anything costly on his cart.

When she put it on, she saw that it was very pretty, the muslin embroidered with flowers of pale blue, echoing the ribbons that crossed over her breast and hung down from her waist at the back.

She knew Nanny must have taken a great deal of trouble over it and, when she ran downstairs, carrying her bonnet in her hand, she went first to the kitchen to say,

"Look, Nanny! The Goose-girl has become a Princess, transformed by her Fairy Godmother's magic wand!"

Nanny turned from the stove to look at Anthea and was well aware of how pretty she looked in the muslin gown, which became her, but she said in her usual tart manner,

"'Fine feathers make fine birds! Now you be careful and don't go turnin' the head of the Vicar!'"

They both laughed at this because the Vicar was nearly eighty and going blind.

In fact one of the things that Harry was going to do when he had time was to suggest to the Marquis, who controlled the purse strings, that he pension off the Reverend Theodosius and appoint a younger man for the Parish.

Anthea ate her breakfast, but her thoughts all the time were away at the Big House, wondering if the Marquis was safe.

She fell sure, however, that if anything had happened to him, Harry would have been back before now to inform them of it.

Putting on the chip-straw bonnet she had worn for two years and which had been retrimmed by Nanny to match her new gown, she set off through the Park for the Church, which was only a very short distance from the Dower House.

It had been built a little earlier than Queen's Hoo and was a perfect example of Tudor architecture, but was unfortunately very much in need of restoration.

Harry wisely had not troubled the Marquis with the needs of the Church until he was satisfied with the house he was to live in.

Nevertheless, after the beauty of Queen's Hoo last night, Anthea could not help noticing how the brickwork needed pointing and the stained glass windows were cracked and had lost some of their panes.

It was possible, if one looked upwards, to see the sun gleaming through the holes in the roof of the Chancel.

As she expected, there were only a few elderly women in the Church and some of the older children who were forced to go by their Sunday School teacher.

The rest of the women would be preparing their Sunday luncheon and like Nanny would therefore attend Evensong.

Anthea moved along a side aisle and made her way to the organ.

It had once been a very fine instrument given by her grandfather soon after he inherited the house, but it had been repaired many times over the years until it was impossible to do any more for it and what was urgently needed was a new organ altogether.

"Do you think that the Marquis will give us one?" Anthea had asked Harry.

He had shrugged his shoulders.

"As I cannot imagine Eaglescliffe going to Church," he said, "I don't think he will be interested in the musical needs of the community. But give me time and I will try to work him around into doing something about it."

"Please do, dearest," Anthea begged him.

She was thinking how wonderful it would be if she could play an up to date really good organ instead of being continually nervous of what sounds would come out of the old pipes that were cracked and often for no reason whatsoever would suddenly cease to function at all.

Now, as she sat down and waited for the small boy who pumped the organ to start doing so, she told herself that there was something she knew, which Harry did not, and that was that the Marquis was musical.

She could still hear his voice praising her playing last night when she was aware that he forgot to drawl in his usual sarcastic manner and had actually sounded quite enthusiastic.

Then, as she remembered how quite unexpectedly he had kissed her, she blushed and concentrated on her playing so that the Vicar would know that she was there and ready when it suited him to leave the vestry with the choirboys.

Then, because she felt happy, she played an unusually elaborate piece of music as the small congregation left the Church to shake the hand of the Vicar at the porch.

It seemed to Anthea as if the organ resounded to her own feelings, but suddenly, while she still had quite a lot more to play, there was a groan, followed by two sharp squeaks and then silence.

"What has happened?" she asked, looking round to where the small boy should have been pumping.

"It wasn't me, miss, it wasn't!" he protested.

'If it was not Timothy,' Anthea thought, 'then it was the organ itself.'

That meant it would have to be repaired, which last time this had happened, had taken a very long time.

She rose reluctantly, feeling that there was nothing she could do about it and as she did so Timothy said,

"I were pumpin', Miss Anthea, I were, honest!"

"I know you were Timothy," Anthea replied. "I suppose it's another breakdown and I will have to see what can be done about it."

"Does that mean you won't be wantin' me this evenin'?" Timothy asked hopefully.

"I think it's unlikely," Anthea replied, "but I will let you know."

She thought that when Harry came back for luncheon she would ask him if he would have a look at the organ to see if he could do anything about it, as he had done on other occasions.

If it proved too difficult for him, that meant they would have to wait until they could get a man from the nearest town to repair it.

It was all rather tiresome and she had the uncomfortable feeling that it was her own fault for trying to extract from the poor old organ more than it was capable of giving and that was why it had collapsed.

'If only we could borrow one of the pianos from Queen's Hoo while it is being repaired,' she thought.

She knew how exciting it would be for her to be able to play as she had last night on an instrument that at her slightest touch translated what was in her mind into sounds that she had never been able to produce before.

'I shall ask Harry if it is possible to have a piano,' she told herself, 'but I will wait until the Marquis has gone back to London.'

She reached the Dower House, peeped into the kitchen to tell Nanny that she was back and found Harry unexpectedly in the study.

She drew in her breath, frightened as she looked at him that he might tell her the bad news that something had happened to the Marquis.

Instead he said in a cheery tone,

"Good morning, Anthea! I hope and pray that everything will go as smoothly today as it did yesterday."

"Was everything – all right – last night?" Anthea asked, feeling that it was almost impossible for her lips to form the question.

Harry grinned.

"I have had no complaints, but I have not seen my Lord and Master yet this morning. I expect, like the rest of the house party, he is still snoring his head off!"

Anthea did not reply.

She was feeling an unutterable relief, remembering that she had heard his valet promising to call the Marquis at eight o'clock, which meant that if he had been killed, his body would have been found by now.

"How did you manage?" Harry was asking. "There were no problems?"

"No, none," Anthea replied.

"Good!"

There was no doubt from the way Harry ejaculated the word that he too was relieved.

Then Nanny called out that luncheon was ready and they went into the small dining room.

While they were eating the roast beef that Nanny had cooked to a turn and the fresh vegetables Jacobs had brought in from the garden, Harry talked of the horses there were now in the stables and which had obviously delighted him.

"I have never seen anything so fine as the teams some of the Marquis's friends brought down from

London," he said. "There are four chestnuts that are perfectly matched, there are bays I would give my right arm to possess and his Lordship arrived with a different team from the one he has driven here before and they are utterly and completely superb. There is no other word to describe them!"

Anthea listened as Harry went on,

"One thing I am determined to have is some more horses I can ride myself and I don't think that the Marquis will mind the expense, seeing how large the estate is and he himself will want to ride when he is down here."

"Do you think he will come here – often?" Anthea asked a little nervously.

Harry laughed.

"That is a question I don't know the answer to."

He was still talking about the horses when, having finished the fruit salad and eaten a little of the cream cheese that Nanny had made, he rose hastily to say,

"I must get back. There is a great deal to see to and I had a message yesterday from Johnson telling me that he had trouble on his farm. If I can, I want to ride out to see what is the matter, so don't be surprised if I am late."

"Nanny will keep dinner hot for you," Anthea answered.

She saw Harry off and, as he hurried towards the stables to fetch his horse, she knew that because he had been so intent on what he was doing himself, he had fortunately made no enquiries as to her movements last night and had just taken it for granted that things had gone as he planned.

She helped Nanny to clear the table, then, knowing that the old woman would have a rest, went into the drawing room to see what the flowers were like.

Those in one of the vases were drooping a little and Anthea went into the garden to pick some more lilac, syringa, and the first buds of a pink rhododendron, which she thought when it was in bloom would look very pretty.

She carried them back into the drawing room and started to rearrange the case on a table in the window.

She was thinking as she did so of a melody she had played last night, hearing it inside her head and longing to feel the keys of the piano under her fingers so that she could transform it into sound.

When the case was completed, she set it down on a small table beside the spinet.

The door of the drawing room opened and she turned her head in surprise, thinking that Nanny must have had a very short rest.

Then, as she saw who was there, she suddenly stiffened into immobility.

The Marquis closed the door behind him and walked slowly across the room towards her, his dark penetrating eyes on her face, which made her feel shy.

As he approached her, Anthea found that it was impossible to move and even more impossible to speak.

She could only look at him, just thinking wildly that he should not be here and he must not know who she is.

Then, as he stood looking down at her, she managed to gasp a little incoherently,

"W-what do you – want?"

The Marquis smiled and for a moment it swept away the cynical lines at the sides of his mouth.

"I quite naturally, Anthea Brooke, wished to thank you for saving my life."

"H-how – did you know it was – me and why are you – here?"

She thought his eyes, which were difficult to meet, were twinkling as he replied,

"I must admit to being rather intrigued when I called on Mr. Meldosio and he told me that he did not have a daughter."

"You – called on Mr. Meldosio?"

"Of course! What did you expect me to do?"

"I-I never thought of that," Anthea stammered. "But you are – safe. I was afraid – terribly afraid that you would not – listen to me."

"You certainly made everything very mysterious," the Marquis answered. "First by disappearing so that I thought that perhaps, after all, I had just dreamed you and you did not really exist."

Anthea made an incoherent little murmur as he went on.

"Then by reappearing by way of what I now realise is a secret passage, you told me that I was about to be murdered by one of my guests!"

As if she felt she needed support, Anthea put out her hand to hold onto the spinet.

"I-I had to – warn you," she said, "because if you had been murdered – it would have been on – my conscience for – ever that I had let – you die."

"I assure you I am very grateful for my life," the Marquis said, "and that is why I am here."

"But you – should not be – here!" Anthea protested a little wildly. "And I cannot – believe that Mr. Meldosio would have – told you who – I was."

"No, he lied most determinedly, if unconvincingly," the Marquis remarked dryly.

"Then how – why – ?"

"When I left him, he assured me that he had no idea who could possibly have taken his place. Then, when I was driving back to the house to send for my manager and ask him whom he had arranged to play so brilliantly and, if I may say so, so professionally, I passed the Church."

Anthea's eyes widened and she glanced up at him and then away again.

"There were sounds coming from the ancient building that so resembled those I had heard last night," the Marquis said, "that after that it was easy."

"W-what – do you mean?"

"I stopped the first person I saw in the village and asked them who played the organ in the Church, and I was told it was Miss Anthea Brooke. I knew already that your Christian name was Anthea and I could hardly believe that there would be two women of the same name in this small village."

Anthea gave a deep sigh.

"So – that is how you – found me."

"That is how I found you," the Marquis confirmed, "but I find it rather strange that my manager, who spoke very eloquently about other parts of the estate, never mentioned that the previous owner and his sister had moved to live in what I am sure is the Dower House."

Anthea gave a little cry of dismay.

"Oh – please," she said, "there is no – point in your knowing this or to – trouble yourself in any way. You have thanked me for – saving your life – but now, please – go back to your party and – forget that I even exist."

The words seemed to tumble over themselves as she spoke. Then, as she looked up at the Marquis pleadingly, he seemed closer to her than he had before.

As he looked into her eyes, she found it impossible to look away.

"Do you really think that is what I can do?" the Marquis asked. "I think, Anthea, we have a great deal to discuss with each other, so shall we sit down?"

Anthea looked around wildly, as if she had forgotten where she was.

Then she said,

"I-I am sorry – it was rude of me – I should have asked you to do so before – but I do not think you should stay."

"As I have every intention of staying," the Marquis replied, "so you must not feel upset about it."

As if he compelled her, Anthea moved from the window towards the fireplace and sat down on the edge of the sofa that stood on one side of it.

The Marquis seated himself in a high-backed chair and crossed his legs, his Hessian boots shining dazzlingly as he did so and seemed very much at his ease.

"Now, let's start at the beginning," he said. "You are Anthea Brooke, and, unless I am very much mistaken, my manager, whom I know as Dalton, is your brother, Lord Colnbrooke."

"Why should you – think – that?" Anthea asked. "Oh – please don't speculate – and pry into things that – do not concern you."

"As it happens, they concern me very closely," the Marquis answered. "And in case you are going to argue with me, Anthea, let me say that I saw a portrait of 'Dalton' when I came into the hall just now."

"That was my father," Anthea murmured, "when he was Harry's age."

"Your brother is very like him, and now I look for it, there is a distinct resemblance between the two of you."

There was silence and then Anthea said,

"Charles Torrington, who sold you Queen's Hoo, thought it would be – embarrassing if Harry asked you to – employ him as your manager – and that is why Charlie told you he knew a – man called 'Dalton' who would fill the post admirably."

She paused and then said beseechingly,

"Please – please – let Harry stay. It has made such a – difference for him to see the – improvements being made to the house – and if we have to go – away and live – somewhere else it would – break his heart."

"I must admit," the Marquis remarked, "I had a suspicion that Dalton was not who he pretended to be, for I could not imagine anyone who was not closely concerned with the house and the estate minding so desperately what was done about it and caring so fervently for the pensioners, the farmers and everyone who is employed here."

"They are – our people," Anthea said, "and it was terrifying to – think that because there was no – money we would have to – desert them and perhaps they would – starve."

"You have made yourselves very comfortable here," the Marquis remarked, looking round the room.

As if Anthea thought that he was accusing Harry of living it up at his expense, she said quickly,

"We have been able to afford to restore this house with the money you paid for Queen's Hoo. Of course the furniture all came from the Big House and also the pictures – but that has – nothing to do with you."

"And yet I suspect you hated me for buying your home over your head."

"Why should you – think that?" Anthea asked.

"Because it is what I would feel myself in the same circumstances," the Marquis answered.

"I-I did hate you – at first," Anthea admitted, "although I knew that it was – unreasonable. Then when I – met you and – realised that you liked music – it was different."

"I have never in my whole life met a woman who played as well as you played last night and whose music made me understand almost as if you were explaining to me in words every note you played."

The Marquis spoke in a deep voice which was different from the tone he had been speaking in previously and Anthea looked at him, then away again, and said,

"How could you – feel like – that?"

"That is what I ask myself," the Marquis replied, "but there is something else I don't know and one of the reasons why I was looking for you today is to ask you who it was you discovered planning to kill me."

Anthea looked at him in surprise. Then as she did so she realised that she had not told him who was coming to his room and, unless he was on his guard, the man who intended to destroy him would try again.

Giving a cry of horror, she exclaimed,

"You must be careful – very careful! He said that you had to die before Wednesday because then your horse would not run in the Derby and his horse would win."

"Now I have an idea who you are talking about," the Marquis said. "You don't know his name?"

"No, but the lady who was to come to your room and – kill you with a – stiletto is called Milly."

The Marquis's lips tightened and Anthea said in an agitated voice,

"He will try again – of course he will try again! Today is Sunday – and he has today, tomorrow and Tuesday – in which to – kill you, for otherwise, as he said – he would probably be taken to the Debtors' Prison."

The Marquis raised his eyebrows.

"I had no idea that Templeton was in such dire straits. At the same time if you had not come back, Anthea, and reappeared in the same mysterious way as you went, I would now be dead."

Anthea shivered.

"I did not want to come – but if you had died – No – I cannot think about it."

"Unfortunately, it is something I have to do," the Marquis said. "But now you have made things very much clearer for me and I am grateful, very grateful,

Anthea, for being alive. What I am wondering is how I can express my gratitude apart from mere words."

"Oh – please – " Anthea said quickly, "all you must do is to go – away and – forget me."

"I have already told you that is impossible," the Marquis replied, "and I think you will find it difficult to forget me."

She looked at him, then her eyelids dropped and her eyelashes were very dark against the whiteness of her skin.

"Please," she said, "you must not – talk like that and will – you not mention to – Harry that I – stayed late last night – and played in the drawing room?"

"Harry would not approve?"

"No, of course not. He would be very angry – very angry indeed. He told me to come – straight home with Nanny the moment I had – finished playing in the – Dining Hall."

"I am rather surprised that he let you do even that," the Marquis remarked dryly.

"He could not help himself," Anthea said quickly. "He learnt only yesterday morning that Mr. Meldosio had hurt his hand and there was no time to find somebody else. In fact there is no one else in the vicinity who can play the piano and there was no time for him to go into town to find a professional pianist."

"So he told you to take Mr. Meldosio's place," the Marquis completed her explanation.

"It was I who thought of it," Anthea said, "and I begged him to be – sensible because he was – afraid if he did not do – exactly as you wished he would – lose his job."

"I see! You should certainly not have played during the *poses plastiques*."

"I could not see them from behind the piano, which was very disappointing," Anthea said, "but I am sure from the applause that they were very beautiful and like the poses – Lady Hamilton captivated the King and Queen of Naples with."

She was aware that the Marquis was looking at her searchingly, almost as if he was surprised at what she had said.

Then, after what seemed a strange silence, Anthea said again pleadingly,

"Harry must never know – that I was so late. He was asleep when I came home and I went up to bed without waking him."

Then, as another thought came near her, she said with even more urgency in her voice,

"You will not – tell him, you will not – say that – "

It was impossible for her to finish the sentence and the Marquis said quietly,

" – that I kissed you?"

"Y-yes. If Harry – knew, he would be – furious and he might – call you out."

"I think that is unlikely," the Marquis said dryly, "and I assure you, Anthea, while I have my faults, I have never yet talked about a woman I have kissed."

He sounded angry and Anthea said,

"I-I am sorry – but I know it was very – wrong and I should not have gone – upstairs when you – asked me to."

She was so distressed as she spoke that she twisted her fingers together and the colour came and went in her face as she turned her head away from the Marquis.

He looked at her for a long moment before he said,

"If it upset you, forget what happened. Just remember that because I was audacious enough, if that is the right word, to take you into my bedroom, it was instrumental in saving my life for, if you had not been there, I should at this moment be lying dead."

"No one will – ever know – that," Anthea said as if she consoled herself.

"Except you and, of course, me," the Marquis agreed quietly. "So what can we do about it, Anthea?"

"Nothing," Anthea said quickly, "and as long as Harry does not know and he can stay here as your manager, everything is perfect."

"Perhaps from your point of view, but not from mine," the Marquis said. "I always pay my debts and I am deeply and irrevocably in your debt, Anthea."

"But those two people may – still try to – kill you."

"'Forewarned is forearmed!'" the Marquis replied. "I assure you that tonight my door will be locked and I cannot believe that anybody other than yourself will enter my room by the secret passage."

"I shall pray that – you will be safe."

"That is what I thought perhaps you would do," the Marquis said, "and I have a feeling that your prayers are always answered."

"I wish that was true – " Anthea began, then she stopped. "No, perhaps you are right – I had not thought of it before – but I prayed and prayed that somehow we could find enough money in order to live at Queen's Hoo. Although the answer to my prayers did not come exactly as I expected, I am here, and Harry is happy because he is looking after what was his own land and house, which looks even more beautiful than he ever imagined it could be."

"That is obviously a point in my favour," the Marquis remarked.

He rose as he spoke and Anthea rose too.

He looked around the room and then said,

"I see you have a spinet, but not a piano. Perhaps the best way I could express my gratitude to you would be to give you a piano."

He saw the answer to his question by the sudden light that came into Anthea's face and seemed to illuminate her large blue eyes and there was an expression almost of rapture in her face.

Then she said falteringly,

"H-Harry would think it – very strange."

"I think I can make him accept it without thinking that I have any ulterior motive in giving it to you personally," the Marquis replied.

"Could you do that? Oh, if you could, it would be absolutely wonderful!" Anthea cried. "And if, as I think, the organ in the Church has to be repaired, then I could play the piano there while the necessary work is done and we would not have to hold the Services without any music."

"Am I to understand," the Marquis asked in a surprised voice, "that the organ I heard you playing so skilfully this morning needs repairing?"

"It broke down again while I was playing it and I would have asked Harry to mention it to you when he had the chance," Anthea said.

The Marquis laughed and it was a sound of genuine amusement.

"I can see that I have taken on a great many things I did not expect when I bought Queen's Hoo for a very different reason."

"Charlie said that it was because it was near to London – and you wanted to give parties for your lady friends whom you could not take to your home."

The Marquis stiffened.

"Charlie should not have said anything like that to you," he said sharply.

"He did not," Anthea confessed. "He was saying it to Harry and was not aware that I was listening – but

I did not think there was anything wrong in that – until last night."

"I asked you, Anthea," the Marquis repeated, "what made you change your mind last night?"

Because she was embarrassed, Anthea moved away and with her back to him looked down at the empty fireplace.

"It was – only," she said in a very small voice, "when I realised – and it seemed very strange – that the ballet dancer or actress – whichever she was – was in bed with the gentleman who wants to – kill you and I don't – think that they are – m-married."

The Marquis was silent until he asked,

"Anything else?"

Anthea did not reply and after a moment he said,

"I think too that you were shocked by my taking you to my bedroom and kissing you."

"I was – very surprised," Anthea said, "because I never thought – I never imagined anyone would want to – kiss someone they did not know – and who had in fact had only spoken to them for a – few minutes."

There was a strange look in the Marquis's eyes before he said,

"I think perhaps my excuse must be that I was carried away by your music. You play very beautifully, Anthea, and, as I have already said, your music told me things about you that made me feel as if I have known you for a very long time."

Anthea turned round.

"Is that – true – really true?"

The Marquis looked probingly into her innocent blue eyes and heard the childlike note in her voice.

"I have a great deal to tell you sometime," he said, "but, as I am sure that you don't wish your brother to know I am here and I have to get back to my house party, I think I should leave you."

"You will – take care of yourself?"

"I have already promised you I will do that, but I am relying on your prayers and you must not forget that they kept me safe last night."

"Perhaps it was Fate or else your Guardian Angel that made me run away along the secret passage," Anthea said as if she was reasoning it out for herself.

"That is something we will talk about another time," the Marquis said. "All I can say now is thank you, Anthea, and we will not worry your brother by letting him know that I have discovered you and the secret of 'Mr. Dalton'."

"You are very kind," Anthea smiled, "and I am very – very – grateful."

She put out her hand as she spoke, and to her surprise instead of shaking it the Marquis raised it to his lips.

As his mouth touched the softness of her skin, she remembered the strange sensations he had given her when his lips had twisted hers and, because she was sure that he was thinking of it too, the colour flooded into her face.

Then abruptly the Marquis turned and walked towards the door.

"I shall be calling on you again, Anthea," he said, "and I will not forget about the piano."

He did not wait for her reply, but went from the room and she heard his footsteps crossing the hall.

He obviously did not expect her to see him off and she thought perhaps it would be wiser to stay where she was.

She was sure that Nanny would not have heard the Marquis arrive, but she might have heard their voices as they spoke to each other and wondered who was there.

Then, as she heard faintly in the distance the sound of wheels driving away, she thought what an extraordinary conversation she had had with the Marquis and how he was different in every way from what she had expected.

There was no doubt that he was intimidating, overwhelming and in fact majestic.

At the same time would anyone else have understood what she had tried to say in her music?

Who else would have understood that Harry's identity must be kept a secret? And that he must never, never know that the Marquis had kissed her.

There was a strange feeling within her breast as she thought of his kiss and she remembered the sensations that like a flash of lightning had swept through her body.

'I must not think about it,' she told herself, 'because if he had realised that I was not 'Miss Meldosio' but Papa's daughter, he would have treated me in a very different way.'

He had not said so, but she knew that was true and she told herself that what had happened was entirely Harry's and her fault in trying to deceive the Marquis.

It would have been better perhaps if they had been frank and open, telling him that Mr. Meldosio had hurt his hand and there could therefore be no music.

But, if they had done that, the Marquis would have died and there would have to be a new owner of Queen's Hoo.

"We are lucky – very lucky to have – him," Anthea murmured.

She thought that the sunshine coming through the window had a special dazzling gold about it that made it quite different from the sun that had shone before the Marquis's arrival.

CHAPTER FIVE

There were a dozen things on Monday morning for Anthea to do in the house, but, although she was busy, she kept thinking with a feeling of relief that today the Marquis's guests would be leaving Queen's Hoo for London and Lord Templeton and Milly would be amongst them.

She had looked in Harry's sporting paper, which he took once a week, and found that there was quite a lot written about Lord Templeton's chance of winning the Derby, but the favourite was a horse belonging to the Marquis.

It was therefore easy to understand that, if the Marquis was dead and his horse therefore did not run, Lord Templeton hoped to win a great deal of money.

But it seemed to her inconceivable that anyone, especially a gentleman, would be prepared to murder another sportsman just because he himself was in debt.

'He is a wicked man!' she told herself.

At the same time it sent a little tremor of fear through her at the thought that he might find some other way of murdering the Marquis, even if it did not mean using the stiletto that he had described to Milly.

She knew how shocked her mother would be to think of such people and also actresses and ballet dancers in particular staying in Queen's Hoo and of her being involved with them.

'They are going away!' Anthea repeated beneath her breath, and she hoped that they would never come back.

Harry arrived home late for luncheon as usual with Nanny fussing because she said that the lamb stew she had cooked for him would be ruined.

As he sat down at the table, he said to Anthea,

"I have news for you!"

"What is it?" she asked.

"It's a surprise that I think will please you."

She waited, half-expecting what he was about to say, and he went on,

"I was clearing away the stage in the Dining Hall this morning, when the Marquis appeared and I said to him,

"'I was wondering, my Lord, where you want this piano put.'

"'I was also thinking about that,' the Marquis replied, 'and actually it is somewhat surplus to our needs.'

"I waited, wondering what he would decide and after a minute he said slowly,

"'Pianos need playing to keep them in good condition. It would be a great mistake for it to be put away in one of the attics. I therefore suggest you ask Miss Meldosio, who played it so skilfully last night, to house it for me until I require it again.'"

As Harry ceased speaking, Anthea drew in her breath.

Then he said sharply,

"How did he know that it was Miss Meldosio who was playing and not her father?"

There was an awkward pause while Anthea thought quickly,

"The Marquis came onto the stage after everybody had left the Dining Hall."

"So that was how he found out!" Harry exclaimed.

Anthea said nothing and after a moment he went on,

"I suppose he was satisfied with your playing. He did not complain?"

"No, he said that it was exactly what he required."

She did not say any more and Harry seemed satisfied, but her heart was singing because the Marquis had found a way to give her the piano.

She knew nothing could be more wonderful than to be able to play it every day or whenever she thought of a melody in her head that she wanted to express with her fingers.

Fortunately Harry had so much to tell her about the trouble at the Jackson farm, which was the result of a fire in the dairy, that he forgot to go on questioning her about what had happened last night.

Only when he had finished luncheon and rose from the table did he say,

"It was nice of you not to wake me when you came home on Saturday night. To tell the truth, I was pegged out, not only with having so much to do but worrying as to whether the Marquis would find everything satisfactory."

Anthea gave a little laugh.

"If you want to know the truth, I think you can consider that everything was perfection. You know how Charlie says he notices every detail and nothing gets past his eagle eye."

"He may be saving it up to give me a telling off before he leaves," Harry said.

His attention was diverted from what he was saying by the sound of wheels outside the front door and he exclaimed,

"This is your piano. I told them to bring it here as soon as there was a cart available."

When the piano had been installed in the drawing room and the spinet removed to another room, Harry left, hurrying back to Queen's Hoo to see if there was anything he could do for the Marquis before he returned to London.

Only when Anthea was alone and she could sit down at the piano and start to play did she say a prayer of gratitude and at the same time a paean of thanks seemed to vibrate from her fingers and echo round the room.

It was late in the day when Harry returned and he hurried straight upstairs to have a bath and change out of his riding clothes, which he had worn all day.

When he came down, Anthea was waiting for him in the drawing room.

"I am sorry I am late," he said, "but everything had to be put aside because, as soon as luncheon was finished, we started to get those women off to London."

He laughed as he said,

"I have never seen such a caboodle! They had all brought enough trunks and bonnet-boxes to last them for months rather than two days!"

"They have all – gone?" Anthea asked.

"All except the Marquis."

Anthea looked at her brother in surprise.

"Why has he stayed behind?"

"I thought he was leaving too," Harry replied, "but apparently he changed his mind. Actually I don't think he is feeling very well."

"Why should you think that?"

Anthea's voice was sharp.

"He looked as if he had a cold and he had a raucous sort of cough."

Anthea did not say anything and after a moment Harry went on,

"He is such a strong athletic chap that I never think of him as having ailments like any ordinary human being."

That was what Anthea thought herself, but she did not say anything.

She only had a terrifying feeling, when Harry had said that the Marquis was not well, that perhaps Lord Templeton had poisoned him in some unsuspected manner.

Then she told herself that perhaps the Marquis was being clever in not going back to London, where Lord Templeton might easily attack him, but instead was staying until Wednesday to go straight to the Derby from Queen's Hoo.

It was just an idea, but she decided not to mention it to Harry.

Instead she played the piano to him after dinner including some of the tunes she knew he liked. Then she realised that he had gone to sleep in the armchair and was no longer listening to her.

She left the piano and woke him up, saying,

"Time for bed, Harry! You are still tired and, if the Marquis has not gone back to London, I am sure that he will have a great deal for you to do tomorrow."

"You may be certain of that!" Harry grinned.

He kissed her outside her bedroom door and went into his own room, where Anthea was sure that he would sleep the moment his head touched the pillow.

She stood for a long time looking out of her window at the stars coming out one by one in the sky and, although she had not made a conscious decision to do so, she was praying that the Marquis would be safe at Queen's Hoo until Wednesday.

When finally she went to bed, she dreamed that she was hurrying down one of the secret passages to find him, but that unseen hands were holding her back and she was struggling frantically against them when she woke up.

She went down to breakfast to find that Harry had already gone and she knew that he would be eager to see that everything continued to go smoothly until the Marquis left.

She therefore ate alone and, when she had finished, she carried the plates and cups back into the kitchen for Nanny to wash up.

"It's goin' to be warm today," Nanny said, "so don't you go tirin' yourself by rushin' about. As soon as I've made the beds I'm goin' down to the village. We're completely out of flour and half-a-dozen other things as well."

"Shall I go for you, Nanny?" Anthea asked.

Nanny refused firmly and Anthea said no more, but was sure that she was, in fact, looking forward to a good gossip in the shops about the goings-on up at Queen's Hoo over the weekend.

She was quite certain that the village would have a great deal to say about it and. as it was the first time that the new owner had been in residence, they would have much to say about him as well.

When Nanny had left, she was wondering whether it would be self-indulgent if she sat down at the piano, when she heard the sound of wheels outside the front door and hurried into the hall.

To her surprise she saw the village doctor, an elderly man of whom she was very fond, having known her all her life, outside in his old-fashioned gig.

When he stepped down from it, Anthea met him on the steps.

"Good morning, Dr. Groves," she greeted him "How lovely to see you."

"You are looking very pretty, Anthea, my dear," he replied, "and very well, thank God!"

They walked into the hall and, as Anthea waited for him to tell her why he had come, after a moment he said,

"Anthea, I need your help."

"Of course," Anthea replied. "Who is ill?"

She thought as she asked the question that it would be one of the pensioners, who were all growing very old and were continually laid up and unable to cook or clean for themselves.

This meant that Anthea or Nanny had to take them something nourishing to eat at least once a day.

To her astonishment the doctor replied,

"It's the Marquis who is in trouble."

Anthea's eyes widened as she asked,

"What has happened to him?"

"He has Spring Fever," Dr. Groves answered, "and, although I have given him something to reduce his temperature, I have nothing on my shelves as good as what your mother used to make and for which I know you have the prescription."

"Yes, indeed," Anthea said, "and I have a bottle upstairs, although, of course, it is best when it is made freshly."

"Spring Fever can be very unpleasant," Dr. Groves went on. "The Marquis is feeling very sorry for himself."

He smiled as if it amused him that such a strong overwhelming man should succumb to a complaint more common amongst the younger people in the village.

"I will go and fetch you what Mama always made up for Spring Fever," Anthea said.

Dr. Groves glanced at the grandfather clock.

"It would be a great help, Anthea," he said, "if you could possibly take it up to Queen's Hoo for me. I have to drive out to the Cosmet farm, which is three miles away, as Mrs. Cosmet is expecting a baby and has already sent me an urgent message to come as quickly as I can."

"I think that will be number seven!" Anthea remarked.

"I have a suspicion it is twins," Dr. Groves said. "In which case it will be number eight as well!"

Then he smiled and added,

"I often think that an ideal family is made up as yours is."

Anthea laughed.

"I am that sure Mama would have liked another son and Papa another daughter."

"Splendid, if she was as pretty as you! One cannot have too much of a good thing!"

He patted Anthea on the shoulder and then went quickly down the steps to climb back into his gig.

"Tell the Marquis's valet exactly how much he should take of your mother's medicine. He seems an intelligent man and will do what you say."

He drove off as he spoke and Anthea waved to him.

Then she ran back into the house and hurried up the stairs.

As she had thought, there was one small bottle of her mother's medicine for Spring Fever, which since her death she had made up whenever it was required.

Dr. Groves was right, she knew, in saying that it was very much better than the standard medicines that he had to prescribe for the same complaint and which she knew usually gave the patients strong indigestion.

She remembered how Harry had said that the Marquis had a cough and she found her mother's special cough syrup, which was made principally of honey infused with two or three special herbs that soothed the throat.

As Anthea had found herself, it swept away a cough almost like magic.

She put the two bottles into a small basket, tied the ribbons of her bonnet under her chin and set off for the Big House.

As she went, she was wondering whether she would have a chance to thank the Marquis for giving her the piano and to tell him what a delight it was.

'I would like to play for him again,' she thought.

She found it very strange that he should understand what she was trying to say when she played her own compositions.

No one else had ever understood, as apparently he did, that she was turning into sound what she saw with her eyes and felt in her heart.

She was sure that none of his friends who had been staying with him these past few days had any idea that he was musical.

It did not take her long to reach Queen's Hoo, but she was deep in her thoughts as she walked through the wood rather than up the drive.

It was only when she was actually there that she saw a phaeton drawn by four horses standing outside the front door.

As she drew nearer, she saw that the horses were sweating and guessed that they had come at a quick pace down from London.

She was quite certain there was no one in their neighbourhood who had such a smart turnout or such magnificent animals.

She walked up the steps into the hall and said to the footman in attendance,

"Could I speak to his Lordship's valet? I have brought on the instructions of Dr. Groves some medicine, which his Lordship should take as soon as possible."

"I'll fetch Mr. Haynes, miss," the footman replied. "Perhaps you'd like to wait in the library."

He walked ahead to open the door into the huge library, which occupied half the centre of the house.

Anthea stared about her with delight, thinking that the brilliant colours of the books were very different from those that had filled the shelves before Harry sold the house.

"I'll go and fetch Mr. Haynes, miss," the footman said.

Then, as he was about to shut the door behind him, Anthea said,

"I see his Lordship has a visitor. Do you know who it is?"

"Yes, miss," the footman replied. "It's Lord Templeton. He has some fine racehorses, I understand."

As he closed the door, Anthea gave a little gasp.

'Lord Templeton – so early in the morning! Why?'

Even as she thought of him, she had a strange premonition of danger for the Marquis, which she felt was menacing him.

She put the basket with the medicine in it down on a table and then she was running as quickly as she could to the very end of the library.

Because it was so large there were two fireplaces and she knew that at the side of the one at the far end there was an opening onto another secret passage that would take her to the Master bedroom.

She ran so quickly that she was breathless by the time she reached it.

Then, as she glanced at the mantelpiece, she saw on either side of a large marble and ormolu clock there were a pair of duelling pistols.

They were obviously there as a decoration, for their handles were embossed with gold and a number of small cabochon emeralds.

Without really thinking, but with a perception and an instinctive awareness that the Marquis's life was threatened, Anthea snatched one of the pistols from the mantelpiece and a second later had opened the door in the panelling.

Inside there was a stepladder rising straight up the side of the wall, which she knew ended on the side of the mantelpiece in the Marquis's bedroom opposite the opening of the secret passage that she had used on Saturday night.

Her father had always said that this was the older of the two passages and had been built at the same time as the house as a protection for its owner against his enemies.

Anthea scrambled up the ladder, aware as she did so that the rungs were dusty and would leave marks not only on her hands but also on her gown.

There was just a faint light from some hidden source when she reached the top that enabled her to see, without having to grope for it, the panel leading into the Marquis's bedroom.

She found the catch easily and then, controlling her breath and the frightened beating of her heart, she opened the secret door very slowly and quietly.

Because the opening was opposite the great canopied bed, she could see at first glance through the crack the Marquis lying back with his eyes closed as if he was asleep.

She thought with a sense of relief that he was alone, until she opened the door a little wider and then stiffened as she saw Lord Templeton standing on the far side of the bed.

He was not looking at the Marquis, as she might have expected but, to her surprise, was taking a pillow from beside him.

Then, carrying it in his hands, he moved past the carved pillars at the end of the bed to stand beside the Marquis.

He had moved slowly and so softly that Anthea thought that he must be walking on tiptoe.

Then, as she watched, thinking his movements were very strange, she realised with horror what he was about to do.

Holding the pillow at each end, he lifted it above the Marquis's head and she knew that he was about to bring it down over his face, thereby suffocating him.

With a sudden gesture she flung the door of the secret panel wide open and, lifting the pistol in her right hand, she called out sharply,

"*Stop!* Stop that immediately!"

Lord Templeton, a thick-set middle-aged man with a red face and greying hair, turned to look at her in astonishment and, although he was holding the pillow over the Marquis's face, he did not press it down as he had intended.

It was then, as he stared at Anthea, that the door from the passage opened and Haynes came in carrying the basket that she had left in the library.

Lord Templeton, however, did not notice him, because his eyes were on Anthea.

"Who are you and what do you want?" he asked.

"If you don't remove that pillow," Anthea threatened, "I will shoot you!"

She was well aware that the pistol was unloaded, but she thought that Lord Templeton would not know that fact and therefore would be afraid that she might carry out her threat.

Then there was a movement from the bed and the Marquis pushed the pillow from his face. As he did so, he raised himself up into a sitting position.

"So you are still trying to kill me, are you, Templeton? I know how you instructed Milly to stab me when I was asleep. Well, this time you have been caught red-handed and I give you twenty-four hours to get out of the country before I prefer charges against you, which will undoubtedly take you to the Old Bailey."

"Charges? What charges?" Lord Templeton blustered, his face growing redder than it was already.

"You were intendin' to suffocate his Lordship!" Haynes said. "I sees you with me own eyes!"

Lord Templeton made a derisive sound, which he intended as a laugh.

"Who would believe such arrant nonsense?" he asked. "I should deny it categorically!"

"You will get out of the country," the Marquis said. "I have had enough of your scheming!"

"Bring your charges *and be damned!*" Lord Templeton stormed. "Nobody would believe the word of a servant and a doxy against mine."

Anthea lowered the pistol she had been pointing at Lord Templeton and stepped through the narrow panel into the room.

"I am perfectly prepared to give evidence against you, my Lord," she said, "and my name is the

Honourable Anthea Brooke, daughter of the late Lord Colnbrooke!"

Lord Templeton stared at her as if he still intended to be defiant.

Then with a growl that sounded like that of an animal he walked across the room towards the door.

"Twenty-four hours, Templeton," the Marquis reiterated, "and I mean what I say."

Lord Templeton did not reply, but merely slammed the door shut behind him.

For a moment there was only silence among the three people left behind.

Then the Marquis said faintly,

"See that he leaves, Haynes, and does not set the house on fire before he does so!"

Haynes, who appeared to have been watching what was happening as if he was in a trance, thrust the basket into Anthea's hand.

Pulling open the door, he left and they could hear him running down the passage after Lord Templeton.

Anthea's thoughts were only for the Marquis.

As if the effort had been too much for him, his eyes were closed and he looked, she thought, almost in a state of collapse.

Quickly she took the pillow that Lord Templeton had intended to smother him with and put it down on the floor.

Then she set her basket on an adjacent table and took out the bottle that contained her mother's prescription.

She had included before she left home a small glass with which her mother measured out the medicine for her patients and which was marked with a diamond cut showing exactly where two tablespoons would reach.

Impatiently, because she felt that it was in the way, Anthea pulled off her bonnet and threw it onto a chair.

Then she filled the small glass up to her mother's mark and, going to the bed, put her arm behind the Marquis's neck to lift him so that he could drink.

His eyes were still closed and she reckoned that he was running a high temperature because his skin felt hot.

And yet he was conscious enough not only to know what had been happening but also to drink from the glass she pressed against his lips.

"This will soon make you feel better," she said soothingly in the same tone that she might have used to a child. "It will bring down your temperature and you will feel more like your usual self."

When the glass was empty, she lowered the Marquis's head back onto the pillow, smoothed the sheets in front of him and, picking up the pillow that Lord Templeton had intended to suffocate him with, carried it round the bed to put it down tidily on the other side.

She came back again to the Marquis and, putting her hand very gently on his forehead, felt that his skin was hot and dry. She knew that with Spring Fever the patient always ran a very high temperature until the fever broke.

She left her hand there for a moment and then the Marquis said faintly without opening his eyes,

"Play – to – me."

It was a request that she was not expecting and she looked around the bedroom as if there would be a piano that she had not previously noticed.

Then she saw the door into the boudoir and, without asking questions, she walked across the room to open the door.

Anthea had not been in the boudoir, which had been her mother's, since the furniture from it had been removed to the Dower House because she loved it sentimentally.

Harry had had the room painted and decorated and the furniture intended for it had been the last among the vanloads to be delivered from London.

She saw now that the room with its white panelling picked out in gold leaf was very beautiful, as was the Louis XIV furniture covered in blue brocade, which matched the elaborately draped curtains over the window.

Then, just inside the communicating door, she saw what she was seeking.

It was a piano and quite the most beautiful she could ever have imagined.

The sides were ornamented with plaques of *Sèvres* china, the blue of which matched the curtains and the feet were elaborate.

She had no idea that a piano could look so exquisite and, as she opened the lid, she could not help wondering, if as it was obviously very old, it would not be rather like the spinet she played at home.

Then she realised that the whole keyboard had been replaced with the same kind of up to date mechanism that now stood in the drawing room at the Dower House.

She sat down, ran her fingers over the keys and knew that only the Marquis could have thought of anything so clever as to renovate an antique piano so cleverly.

Now she could thank him in music, as she wanted to do in words, for what he had given her.

She played first of all what she was sure he would recognise as her thanks for a present that was more important to her than anything else he could have thought of.

The gentlemen who had been the Marquis's guests on Saturday night might have given the ballet dancers and the actresses who accompanied them diamond necklaces and jewels of all descriptions, but Anthea knew that she would rather have a piano than anything else in the whole world.

She told the Marquis this through the music and then went on to say that he must hurry up and get well.

There was sunshine outside, the birds were singing in the trees and there was so much on his new estate for him to see and explore.

She tried to describe the small streams where there were fish, which her father had sometimes brought home for them to enjoy at breakfast and the fields where there would be partridges in the autumn, as there would be pheasants in the woods.

There were still deer to be found in the Park, although they had grown fewer and fewer during the years when her father did not replace them.

There were also the little red squirrels with their fluffy tails, who hid their stores of nuts in the hollow parts of the oak tree.

She played almost everything she loved, which, because they meant so much to her, she wanted the Marquis to love too.

'It is all yours,' she tried to tell him, 'and I know and you must understand that it all needs your attention and affection as much as do the old people in the cottages and the children who can go to school only if you pay for a teacher to instruct them.'

There was so much she wanted to say to him that she had played for quite a long time before she realised that Haynes was standing by her side.

She looked up at him enquiringly and took her hands from the keyboard.

"His Lordship's asleep, miss," he said in a whisper, "and I think the fever has broken."

Hastily Anthea rose to her feet and entered the bedroom.

Haynes was right.

Now there were beads of sweat on the Marquis's forehead and when, very gently, so as not to disturb him, she felt his pulse, she knew that his temperature had fallen and the skin on his wrist was not as hot as it had been.

She went back into the boudoir, beckoning Haynes to follow her.

"As soon as his Lordship wakes," she said in a low voice, "give him another glass of the mixture I brought him and persuade him, if possible, to gargle with what is in the pot, which will take away his cough."

Haynes nodded to show that he understood and Anthea went on,

"I will go home now and bring back some fresh medicine for the fever, which will take him through the night. You will be with him?"

She had a sudden fear that Lord Templeton might come back secretly and try again to kill the Marquis.

She could not really believe that he would tamely go abroad because the Marquis had threatened him.

"I won't leave his Lordship," Haynes whispered, "and if that murdering devil comes near him, I'll fill him so full of lead he'll not live to see another day!"

The way he spoke told Anthea how deeply devoted Haynes was to his Master and she gave him a smile as she put on her bonnet, which she had picked up as she left the bedroom and tied the ribbons under her chin.

Haynes handed her the empty basket and she left the boudoir by the door that opened into the passage.

She was wishing that she could look at the Marquis once again, but she was afraid that Haynes might think it strange.

She hurried home, knowing that she was very late for luncheon and that Nanny would be wondering what had happened to her.

She knew she could not explain either to her or to Harry that she had been saving the Marquis's life for the second time.

And yet incredibly, unbelievably, that was what she had done!

chapter six

It took Anthea a long time to make the new medicine for the Marquis.

At first she thought that she could not find the right herbs in the Dower House garden and would have to go up to Queen's Hoo to where in the past her mother had always grown them.

Fortunately, however, she found just a few tucked away in a corner where she had not noticed them at first.

After she had cut them up and put together all the ingredients her mother had insisted upon, it was growing quite late in the afternoon.

She, however, walked quickly through the beech wood, hoping that Harry would not see her and, when she reached the front door of Queen's Hoo, she asked for Haynes.

She was shown once again into the library and now she had time to look around and think how perfect it was and exactly how a library should be.

She wished that she could read all the books there, which she was sure were far more up to date than those they had removed to the Dower House.

She did not have to wait long before Haynes appeared.

"I was expectin' you, miss," he said almost reproachfully, "because I've given his Lordship the last drop in the bottle you gave me."

"How is his Lordship?" Anthea enquired.

"Sleeping peacefully, miss, and I was just wonderin' if you would want me to wake him up to take another dose as soon as you arrived with it or whether I should just leave him be."

"Shall I come to have a look at him?" Anthea suggested.

"Yes, of course, miss."

Haynes escorted her up the stairs and along the passage and, when they entered the Master bedroom, Haynes went ahead very quietly to see if the Marquis was still asleep.

Anthea would have waited in the doorway, but he beckoned and she moved across the thickly carpeted floor to the bedside.

As Haynes had said, the Marquis was fast asleep and, as soon as she looked at him, Anthea could see that he was better.

Very gently she put her hand on his forehead and found it was cool and his skin no longer as dry as it had been when the fever was raging.

Then, as she looked down at him, she found herself thinking that he was not the frightening, overwhelming, magnificent Marquis of whom she, like everybody else, was afraid, but just a young man struck down by a fever and lying like one of the oak trees being felled in the Park.

As she looked at him, she thought that the cynical lines were no longer obvious at the sides of his mouth, in fact there was a faint smile on his lips.

She wondered if she would ever know what had made him what he was, what perhaps had disillusioned him so that he did not find the world as wonderful and exciting as she did.

Then, as she turned away from the bed, and walked towards the door where Haynes was waiting, she had the feeling, although, of course, it was absurd, that the Marquis was after all only a little boy, who needed to be loved and cosseted because he was feeling ill.

She went out into the passage and, as Haynes joined her and closed the door, she said,

"His Lordship is much better. Give him the same medicine as soon as he wakes up and again last thing tonight because it will help him sleep."

"You've got somethin' magic in them herbs of yours, miss," Haynes said. "I've never seen anyone get better from a fever as quick as his Lordship has!"

"Don't speak too soon," Anthea warned. "And it is important that he should not get up too quickly or do too much too soon."

She remembered her mother saying this over and over again one spring, when, after a particularly severe winter, there had been an epidemic of fever in the village and everybody seemed to want her mother's special treatment at the same time.

"I'll try and carry out your orders, miss," Haynes said with a grin, "but you knows what his Lordship's like. If he wants to do somethin', nothing'll stop him!"

"I expect he will feel a little limp tomorrow," Anthea said. "Just try to keep him quiet and persuade him to sleep as much as possible."

"You'd better come back to tell him that yourself, miss."

Anthea laughed.

"I don't suppose his Lordship would listen to me!"

"I wouldn't be all that surprised if he did!" Haynes answered. "After all, you saved his life, for if you'd not seen what Lord Templeton was up to, we'd now be preparin' for his funeral!"

Anthea shivered.

"Don't talk about it," she said. "I only hope he has left England as his Lordship told him to do."

"If you ask me, he'll be too frightened to stay," Haynes said. "At the same time, I ain't takin' no chances. I'd a loaded pistol with me all last night."

They reached the top of the stairs and Anthea stopped.

"Are you quite certain that you can manage to stay up with his Lordship again tonight?" she asked. "It is only that I shall be very nervous about what Lord Templeton might do until after Wednesday."

"Don't you worry," Haynes said. "I'll let no one hurt his Lordship, you can be certain of that! We've been together in some tight spots one way or another and he's always come out on top."

"I hope you are right," Anthea answered. "But, as you say, we must take no chances."

She said goodbye to Haynes and walked back through the Park.

The shadows were growing long and the birds were going to roost.

She thought how beautiful and peaceful it was and how it seemed impossible to think that there were men like Lord Templeton in the world who were prepared to kill just for the sake of money.

Then, as she realised that it was growing late, she ran the last fifty yards to the Dower House, being afraid that Harry would be waiting and she would have to explain where she had been.

It was not that she minded telling him, as she intended to do, that Dr. Groves had asked her for her mother's special prescription for Spring Fever.

What she did not want was Harry questioning her as to whether she had seen the Marquis and suspecting that now he was not for her just the new owner whom she had heard of with fear and perhaps hatred, but someone who in a strange way mattered to her because their new relationship was so very unexpected.

'As I have saved his life twice,' Anthea argued to herself, 'I can hardly be expected to feel indifferent as to whether he lives or dies in the future.'

Then she knew that this was something she did not wish to say to her brother.

To her relief there was only Nanny in the house to scold her for being away for so long.

"I should have thought that his Lordship with all his money could pay for doctors to look after him rather than rely on you!" she muttered.

"But you know as well as I do, Nanny, that Mama's herbal medicines are very much better than anything that Dr. Groves can prescribe."

"Then what's wrong with London doctors?" Nanny asked truculently. "From all I hears, His Royal Highness consults them often enough."

Anthea laughed.

"I cannot believe that the Marquis is often ill," she said. "In fact this must be an exceptional experience for him. Equally, as you well know, Spring Fever is no respecter of persons."

"Well, just be careful you don't catch it yourself!" Nanny warned. "I've got enough to do without nursin' you or Master Harry for that matter!"

She stalked away into the kitchen as she spoke and Anthea knew her truculence was only because she was worried and cared so deeply for her two 'children', as she called them, that anything that threatened their wellbeing made her apprehensive.

By the time Harry returned, Anthea had changed into the simple muslin gown that she always wore at dinner and, when they sat down to enjoy it, Harry had a great deal to tell her about the fire that had taken place on the farm and which necessitated, he was quite sure, building a whole new dairy, as the old one was past saving.

This occupied his mind until they went to bed and the next morning he was in such a hurry to get back to Queen's Hoo that he ate his breakfast saying as little as possible.

When he had gone, Anthea wondered if she also could go up to the Big House and ask for news of the Marquis.

Then, since Harry would be there, she thought it would be a mistake.

She knew that, if his Lordship was indeed worse, Haynes would send for her.

At the same time it was frustrating and she moved about the house worrying about somebody she could not see.

One thing was quite certain, that if, as she expected, she had to make more of her mother's herbal medicine before the Marquis was completely well, she would have to go to the Herb Garden at Queen's Hoo, for there were not enough herbs in their own.

She was still wondering indecisively what would be best when Harry came home early for luncheon.

Because she could not restrain her curiosity, Anthea ran to the front door to meet him, saying as she did so,

"How is the Marquis? Is he better?"

"I think so," Harry replied indifferently. "In any case he is still in his room and I have not seen him."

"Surely you asked?" Anthea persisted.

"If he is well enough, he will be sending for me to give me his orders," Harry replied, "and, as I have a great number of things that still want doing, I can assure you, Anthea, it is a relief to be on my own for a time."

Anthea knew how he felt. But she told herself that, whatever Harry might think, she would go up to Queen's Hoo this afternoon.

They were just finishing the light luncheon that Nanny had prepared for them when there was the sound of wheels outside and Harry looked up to say,

"I wonder who that is!"

A moment later the dining room door was flung open and Charles Torrington walked in.

"Good Heavens, Charlie!" Harry exclaimed. "I was not expecting to see you!"

"I have something to tell you," Charlie said, putting down on a chair the tall hat he had been wearing when he walked straight into the house.

The way he spoke made both Anthea and Harry look at him anxiously and Harry said,

"Sit down and have a drink, unless you would like something to eat?"

"I will in a minute," Charlie replied, "but first I have to tell you why I have come posting here in what I am certain is record time."

He spoke in such a serious voice that neither Anthea nor Harry said anything as Charlie pulled out a chair from the table and sat down.

Then he looked at Anthea and said,

"I don't know quite how to tell you this, Anthea, and I am afraid that it will upset you."

"Oh, come on, Charlie!" Harry exclaimed, "Stop playing about and tell us what is wrong. It must be something pretty bad or you would not be here without any warning."

As he spoke, Anthea, realising that Charlie was still looking at her, felt a streak of fear running through her veins.

"What is – it?" she asked in a low voice.

"I don't suppose you have ever heard of a man called Lord Templeton," Charlie said, "but Harry will know who I mean."

Anthea clenched her fingers together and went very pale, but she did not speak, and Charlie went on,

"He is a blustery, hard-drinking man for whom I have never had any liking and everybody in White's has known for some time he has been gambling for high stakes and his creditors are pressing him."

"What has that to do with Anthea?" Harry interposed.

"I am coming to that," Charlie replied.

There was a little pause before he continued,

"Last night, I understand, Templeton was at White's and drinking himself insensible. But before he was carried out, he announced to a number of members who were there, some of whom are my friends, that he was being driven out of England by the completely untrue and slanderous accusations that Eaglescliffe had levelled at him. He said that they were substantiated only by a young woman he found in the Marquis's bedroom who had pointed a pistol at him and threatened to take his life."

Anthea drew in her breath because she knew what was coming next.

"Templeton swore," Charlie went on in a very serious tone, "that the young woman's name was Anthea Brooke, the sister of Harry Colnbrooke."

As Charlie finished speaking, Harry brought his fist down hard on the table.

"Of all the ridiculous nonsense I have ever heard, this is the worst!" he raged. "How dare Templeton say such things about Anthea? He must have the name wrong, but I will make him publicly retract his lies and the quicker the better!"

"That is exactly what I thought when I heard about it," Charlie agreed, "but the extraordinary thing is that Templeton has withdrawn his horse from the

Derby and, if my friends are to be believed, has gone abroad."

"What for? Why?" Harry asked. "Wherever he has gone, I will follow him to make him eat his lies and clear Anthea's name if it is the last thing I do!"

He spoke furiously and, as if she could not bear what was happening any longer, Anthea rose from the table and, without saying a word to Harry or Charlie, walked out of the room.

As she closed the door she heard Harry say,

"Now, look here, Charlie, this has to be stopped – "

She did not wait to hear anything more, but ran out of the front door and without thinking, without even considering it, started to run through the path in the wood which was the shortest way to Queen's Hoo.

She could think of only one person who could help, one person who would understand.

But before she said anything, before she told Harry what had really happened, she knew that she must ask the Marquis what would be the best way to inform her brother of what she realised now he should have been told as soon as it had happened.

'Why did I try to keep it a secret?' she asked despairingly.

Then she knew that the answer was quite simple – it would have been impossible to tell Harry that the Marquis had taken her up to their father's room and kissed her and that then, because she had been frightened, she had managed to escape from him down the secret passage.

The more she thought about what had occurred, the more she found it impossible to know how she could explain it plausibly to her brother as a series of events that had followed one upon the other, until she had saved the Marquis first from being stabbed with a stiletto and then from being suffocated by Lord Templeton.

'What – shall I do? What shall I – do?' she asked herself frantically as she ran.

She felt that only the Marquis could find a solution to what seemed an unanswerable problem.

It was only when she reached the end of the trees and had just a short way to go that she moved a little more slowly and tried to control the breath that came fitfully from between her lips because of the speed at which she had run.

Then, as she walked up the steps to the front door, aware that she had come just as she was, without a bonnet on her head and with her hair curling riotously around her forehead, she managed with an almost superhuman effort to walk in through the open door with dignity.

"I have to see his Lordship immediately!" she said to the footman.

It was the same man who had fetched Haynes for her and he smiled as he said,

"Of course, miss. Mr. Haynes is upstairs with his Lordship, so perhaps you'll like to go up?"

"Thank you," Anthea replied.

The footman went ahead of her and she was still fighting to control her breath as she followed him.

They walked along the corridor to the Master bedroom and, when the footman knocked on the door, Haynes opened it.

There was no need for the footman to say anything as Haynes came out to say,

"It's nice to see you, miss, and I've got a surprise for you!"

"I want to – see his – Lordship!" Anthea said in a voice that did not sound like her own.

"Yes, of course," Haynes agreed, "and I knows his Lordship'll be pleased to see you, seein' how much he owes you."

He did not wait for her reply, but went back into the room, leaving her standing in the doorway, and announced,

"Miss Anthea, my Lord, and just at the right moment!"

It was then that Anthea saw that the Marquis was not in bed as she expected, but sitting in an armchair by one of the windows.

The window was open and the sunshine was pouring in on his dark head and, with the frill of his nightshirt white above the collar of his robe of dark blue velvet, he looked almost as if he were fully dressed.

He certainly looked very different, she thought, from the man she had seen yesterday weak and prostrate against his pillows.

She stood just inside the room for a moment looking at him. Then, as she heard Haynes close the door and she knew that they were alone, she ran towards his chair and stood beside him for a moment, finding it hard to speak.

Then the words came tumbling out.

"Something – terrible has – happened and I need your – help – I need it desperately!"

The Marquis put out his hand as he asked,

"What has occurred? What has upset you?"

Anthea took his hand and without thinking went down on her knees beside his chair.

She clasped the Marquis's hand as if it was a lifeline and she felt the strength of his fingers give her the courage that she vitally needed.

"It is – Lord Templeton," she said a little incoherently as she realised that the Marquis was waiting for her to speak.

The Marquis's fingers tightened on hers.

"What has that swine done to you?" he demanded.

"He has gone – abroad," Anthea said, "as you – told him to do – but last night he said at – White's that you had – forced him to leave the country by making lying and slanderous accusations against him."

The Marquis gave a little laugh.

"He was bound to say something like that."

Then, as he saw in Anthea's frightened, beseeching eyes that this was not the end of the story, he asked,

"What else did he say?"

"He – said," Anthea replied, and her voice was hardly above a whisper, "that he had – found me in your bedroom – and I had threatened to – shoot him."

"He gave your name?" the Marquis asked sharply.

"Y-yes – to quite a number of people – some of whom are Harry's and Charlie's friends."

The Marquis's lips tightened and he was frowning as he said,

"Templeton was always an outsider, but this is completely and absolutely abominable!"

"I-I don't mind it – being said in – London," Anthea faltered, "it is – just that I don't know – how to tell Harry the truth and I am – afraid he will never forgive me if he learns that I was – in your bedroom – in the first place."

The Marquis did not speak and after a moment Anthea said,

"Help me – please – help me. I know it's not very – important to you – but Harry is the – only person I have left in my family – the only person in the whole world who – loves me and I cannot – I cannot lose his love."

As she spoke, because she was so upset, the tears overflowed in her eyes and ran down her cheeks.

The Marquis looked at her and she had the feeling that he was choosing his words very carefully before he said,

"Now, listen, Anthea, we have to be very clever about this and you were quite right to come to me for help. What did you say to Harry and his friend before you left?"

"I did not say – anything," Anthea replied. "We had just finished luncheon when Charlie arrived – and when he told us what Lord Templeton had said about me I jumped up and – ran away to – you."

"That was very sensible," the Marquis said, "and because you have been so sensible, I know that we can find a way out of this mess that will not make Harry angry."

"He will be – very angry that I was in your bedroom – and also very angry that I had – met you without – telling him."

"Do you mean to say that he does not even know we have seen each other?" the Marquis asked incredulously.

"Harry knows that you spoke to – 'Miss Meldosio' and it – was because of that that you asked her to house the piano – and I have not had time to – thank you."

"I don't want your thanks," the Marquis said, "but I thought that my solution to the problem was rather ingenious."

"It was very clever, but Harry thinks that is the only time I have – spoken to you – and he does not know that I played in the – drawing room."

"I see – " the Marquis nodded slowly.

"He was asleep when I came home on Saturday night and Nanny promised not to tell him how late we were."

"I am beginning to see that this is a somewhat more complicated situation than I had thought," the Marquis remarked.

"Please – please," Anthea begged, "tell me what to do – and now I think of it – I am sure that Harry will be very – surprised that I have come here to you."

"I think," the Marquis said after a moment, "that we shall have to make a clean breast of the fact that it was your courage that saved my life. Equally we can perhaps trim the story so that it will not upset your brother as you are afraid it will."

"Please – we cannot tell him – that you – *kissed me*," Anthea whispered.

She could not look at the Marquis as she spoke because it made her feel so shy.

Then he said very quietly,

"No, of course not. That is something entirely personal that concerns only you and me, Anthea."

This in itself was such a relief that she put her head down for a moment against his knee, releasing her hold on his hand as she did so.

"It's all right," he said. "We will get ourselves out of this difficulty just as you saved me from being stabbed to death by Milly and from being suffocated by Templeton."

Anthea raised her head.

"How – can we do – that?"

"You had better leave it to me," the Marquis said. "I have a feeling and I am sure I am right, Anthea, that you are a very bad liar and that your eyes, if not your lips, will always tell the truth."

It seemed such a strange thing for him to say that Anthea stared at him as he went on,

"What I think we must do is send a message to your brother and Charles Torrington asking them to come here immediately. When they do, I will tell them how brave and courageous you have been and how deeply grateful I am to you that I am still alive."

"H-Harry will be – angry – " Anthea began.

"Not if I am clever, as I intend to be," the Marquis interrupted. "Now what I want you to do is to go into the next room and play the piano. I know it will soothe away your fears and I hope too that it will tell you to trust me."

Anthea drew in a deep breath.

"You – really think it will be – all right?"

"I know it will," the Marquis replied. "Just do as I say and remember, as I am your patient, I must not be upset or argued with!"

Knowing that he was trying to make her laugh, Anthea managed a watery little smile.

Then, because the tears were still on her cheeks, the Marquis took a white linen handkerchief, which smelt of *eau de cologne*, from the pocket of his robe.

Bending forward, he wiped her tears away.

She did not think that it was a strange thing for him to do. In fact it seemed completely natural and she was feeling exhausted by her wild dash to Queen's Hoo and the agitation and fear that had upset her.

Now for a moment she did not even want to play the piano.

She just wanted to stay by the Marquis and feel that, because he had taken charge, there was no need for her to worry.

At the same time she could not help remembering that, as she never went to London, if her reputation was ruined it was of no consequence.

But Harry, when he had the time and could afford it, would want to go to White's and it would be intolerable for him to think his sister was being sneered at.

'How can the Marquis put it – right?' she worried.

As if she had asked the question aloud or he could read her thoughts, he said,

"Now, suppose you trust me, Anthea. Surely, because so many strange and unusual things have happened in which we have both been involved, you can understand that this is not an unmanageable problem but one which, as it happens, I will solve, and I am sure that the solution will make you happy. Do you believe me?"

"I-I want to believe you," Anthea answered, "but it is – difficult."

"Now do as I say," the Marquis said as if he was speaking to a small child. "Go into the boudoir and go on playing as you did yesterday, telling me what is happening in the woods outside, in the fields, the Park, and how important I am to the people in the village who look to me to make them happy, as you want them to be."

Anthea's eyes widened and she sat back on her heels as she asked,

"H-how did you know I was – telling you that?"

The Marquis smiled.

"I thought by this time you understood that I know what you are saying in your music, which other people would say in words."

"No one has ever done that before."

"Then I am the first," the Marquis said, "and that is what I want to be."

She felt somehow that there was a further meaning behind what he said.

Then, because she wanted to obey him, she rose slowly to her feet to stand looking down at him, her eyes very large in her small face, her eyelashes still wet with tears.

"It's going to be all right," the Marquis said quietly.

"B-but – I am afraid," Anthea said. "I am still afraid that – Harry will be very angry and perhaps do something stupid like – pursuing Lord Templeton to France – or wherever he has gone – and c-calling him out."

"If anyone fights Templeton, it will be me!" the Marquis said firmly. "But frankly I don't think that he is worth the effort or even the expenditure of a good bullet!"

There was something in the way he spoke that told Anthea that, although he had been comforting her, he was extremely angry at Lord Templeton's behaviour and at the fact that he had besmirched her name in public.

There was, however, she thought, nothing she could do and she merely said,

"Thank you – I do so hope it will be – all right."

"It will be," the Marquis said positively.

As he spoke, he rang the little gold bell that was standing on a table beside his chair and as Haynes appeared he said,

"Send somebody as quickly as possible to the Dower House and ask Mr. Dalton and Major

Torrington to come here immediately. I wish to see them."

"Very good, my Lord," Haynes said, "but you know as well as I do that Dr. Groves said you should be quiet and see no one today."

As the Marquis was speaking, Anthea had moved across the room and had now reached the door into the boudoir.

She turned round to say,

"If this is too much for you, it must wait until tomorrow."

"It's not too much for me," the Marquis replied, "but I think I shall prescribe myself a somewhat stronger tonic than anything you have brought me."

Anthea stiffened.

"It is very selfish of me to – think only about myself," she said, "and I am sure it is time for you to have another dose of the herbal medicine."

"You're quite right, miss!" Haynes agreed. "His Lordship, as it happens, is a quarter-of-an-hour over the time and I've got it ready for him."

"Your magic brew has been very efficacious in sweeping away my fever," the Marquis said. "At the same time, Haynes, when you have carried out the order I have just given you, I want a glass of champagne."

"Very good, my Lord."

Haynes hurried through the door that led to the passage, while Anthea lingered.

"If I have upset you and made you ill again," she said, "I shall be very – very worried."

"Are you really concerned for me?"

"Of course I am!" Anthea replied. "How, having saved you twice from the wicked Lord Templeton, could I allow you to be ill over something that I suppose in reality is very – trivial?"

"I don't think anything that concerns you, Anthea, is trivial," the Marquis said, "and, as this concerns us both, it is in fact very important – to me."

Because he was being so kind she smiled at him and then she said,

"I will thank you in music – which is very much easier."

As she spoke, she went into the boudoir and sat down at the piano.

She wanted, because she was still agitated and still frightened of what Harry would say, to express her anxiety in music, which was disturbing and at the same time somewhat sombre.

Then she told herself that she must think of the Marquis.

He had asked her to play in the same way that she had played to him yesterday and, because she thought that she did trust him and did believe he would help her as he had promised, she must do what he wished.

As she thought of him, she found herself expressing what she thought about him in a melody that would, she felt, make him also understand how grateful she was to him.

'If he was not there, I should be frantic,' she told herself.

But, because in fact he was there and better in health than she would have hoped, the room seemed to be filled with sunshine.

The music blended with the sun and became a prayer flying up into the sky to evoke the Divine Power that could sweep away fear and evil, and make everything, as it should be, beautiful.

Chapter Seven

Anthea continued to play the piano until she heard her brother's voice and then Charles Torrington's greeting the Marquis in the other room.

She waited until she thought that Haynes would have brought chairs for them so that they were seated opposite the Marquis.

Then, as she stopped playing, she heard the Marquis say to Haynes,

"Ask Miss Brooke to join us."

She came in from the boudoir uncomfortably aware that Harry was scowling. She dared not look at him, but sat down in a chair beside him, conscious that her heart was beating frantically because she was frightened.

"I have asked you to come here, Colnbrooke," the Marquis said, speaking directly to Harry, "because I think that you should be informed of the brilliant way that your sister saved my life."

Harry did not speak, and the Marquis went on,

"How it happened was that after she had been playing as 'Miss Anthea Meldosio' on Saturday night she overheard by chance one of my guests, Lord Templeton, planning with a young woman called Milly that she would kill me while I was asleep."

"Good God!" Charlie ejaculated.

The Marquis, however, still speaking to Harry, continued,

"Quite rightly your sister informed me of what she had overheard. While I found it almost too fantastic to believe, I was aware that Templeton was deeply in debt and the only way he could save himself was if my horse was withdrawn from the Derby on Wednesday, as it would be in the event of my death.

"Because, however, your sister had been so insistent that what she had overheard was true, I locked my door when I went to bed and there was no doubt that somebody tried to enter during the night."

"It seems incredible!" Harry muttered.

"That is what I thought," the Marquis agreed, "but I realised that your sister had been brave enough to save my life and I am naturally extremely grateful."

"She should have told me what happened."

Harry looked accusingly at Anthea as he spoke.

She could not meet his eyes, but turned her face away from him to look out of the window as if she sought comfort from the sunshine.

"I am quite certain, 'Miss Meldosio' would have done so," the Marquis said, emphasising the name, "if I had not extracted her promise that she would keep to herself what she had overheard. I am sure that you can understand that if it had been a figment of her imagination, I might have been in a very embarrassing position with my guests."

Harry nodded as if he understood and the Marquis said,

"As you are aware, on Monday morning I tried to show my appreciation of Miss Anthea Meldosio's action by telling you to give her the piano she had played on on Saturday night."

Anthea felt Harry stiffen and knew that he was very angry at having been kept in ignorance.

"However, later on that day, as you are aware," the Marquis went on, "I was struck down by Spring Fever. Dr. Groves said that your mother's herbal remedy was very much more efficacious than any medicine he could prescribe and he would therefore ask Miss Anthea Brooke to make some for me."

"So that is how you guessed who she was!" Harry exclaimed.

The Marquis's eyes twinkled.

"I must admit I had had my suspicions that you were no ordinary estate manager! But to continue, the moment I was given the herbal medicine my fever decreased and Haynes informed me that Miss Anthea Brooke would be bringing a fresh supply on Tuesday morning."

Harry glanced at Anthea again as if he was wanting to ask her why she had not told him about the herbs, but he did not speak and the Marquis went on,

"Your sister arrived in the morning and asked to see Haynes. Her curiosity was aroused by a phaeton and horses drawn up outside and, as she was shown into the library, she asked the footman who was visiting me, knowing that on Dr. Groves's instructions I was supposed to be kept quiet.

"When the footmen informed her that it was Lord Templeton's phaeton that stood there, she realised that once again my life was in danger."

"That was very intelligent of you!" Charles exclaimed, as if he realised that the Marquis's story was very uncomfortable for Anthea and he wanted to reassure her.

"That is what I thought," the Marquis agreed, "because she ran to the fireplace at the end of the library, seized one of the duelling pistols put on the mantelpiece as a decoration and then hurried up to my room by a secret stairway that I had no idea existed."

He spoke a little reproachfully, as if he thought that he should have been informed of it when he became the owner of Queen's Hoo.

Then his voice seemed to deepen as he went on,

"Your sister, Colnbrooke, peeping through the panel by the fireplace, saw me in bed asleep while Templeton was in the act of putting a pillow over my face, intent on suffocating me!"

"I can hardly believe he would do such a thing!" Harry gasped.

"She cried out to him to stop what he was doing," the Marquis continued, "and her voice awoke me at the same moment as Haynes came into the room with the herbal medicine he had found downstairs in the library.

"It took a tremendous effort, for I was very weak, to push the pillow away from my face, but I did so and accused Templeton of trying to kill me for the second time.

"I told him if he did not leave England within twenty-four hours, I would charge him with attempted murder and have him brought to the Old Bailey."

"So that is how it happened!" Harry murmured. "But, Anthea – "

"Your sister," the Marquis interrupted, "heard Templeton say that no one would believe such a story and, when I replied that there were two witnesses, he answered that no Judge would accept the evidence of 'a servant and a doxy'!"

His voice was very positive as he finished,

"It was then that your sister told him who she was and he knew that he was defeated."

"It's the most appalling story I have ever heard," Charles cried. "The man must be insane!"

"That is what I thought myself," the Marquis agreed. "At the same time, I am very grateful to be alive."

"At the expense of my sister's reputation," Harry said bitterly. "I will follow him to France or wherever he has gone and kill him if it is the last thing I do!"

Harry spoke so violently that Anthea clasped her hands together and turned as if to expostulate with him.

"I think that would be a mistake," the Marquis said. "I will make sure that Templeton will not return by laying the information on which the magistrates are bound to issue a warrant for his arrest. I will also make certain that your sister's reputation is not damaged."

"I don't see how you can do that!" Harry said sharply.

The Marquis sat back in his chair and closed his eyes.

"I have a very good answer to that question," he replied, "but, as I am feeling somewhat exhausted, would you permit it to wait until tomorrow?"

Anthea jumped to her feet.

"You have been talking for much too long," she said. "Mama always said that anyone who has Spring Fever must be kept completely quiet for at least twenty-four hours after the fever breaks."

She turned her head towards her brother.

"Please, Harry, go away now. You can see it has all been too much for his Lordship."

Harry was aware as the Marquis sat with his eyes closed that he did look ill and he rose a little reluctantly from his chair.

"Thank you very much, my Lord," he said. "I am very grateful for your explanation and I do hope that you really will be able to repair the damage done by Lord Templeton to my sister."

The Marquis did not reply, but Haynes, who Anthea was quite certain had been listening at the door, came hurrying into the room to say,

"I've got to get his Lordship into bed. It's the rest he needs and all this talkin' does nobody no good!"

No one demurred, but Anthea, following Harry and Charlie to the door, gave Haynes a little smile as she passed him.

When they stood back for her to leave first, she longed to ask if she could stay with the Marquis, but knew that, if she did so, it might make things worse than they were already between her and Harry.

They walked along the corridor in silence until they reached the hall and went out through the front door, where Anthea saw the Marquis's open chaise waiting to carry them back to the Dower House with a coachman and a footman on the box.

They climbed in, Harry and Anthea sitting on the back seat with Charlie opposite them and only when they drove away did Charlie say,

"I think I am dreaming! Nothing we have heard seems real, but straight out of a book."

"I am sorry if you are angry, Harry," Anthea said in a small voice, "but his Lordship made me promise not to tell anyone what I had overheard."

"I suppose you had to do as he asked," Harry admitted. "But the whole business is disgraceful and something I did not expect to happen at Queen's Hoo, of all places!"

"At the same time you have to admit, Harry," Charlie interposed, "that Anthea behaved with tremendous courage and great presence of mind. If she had not saved the Marquis's life, as he said, twice, he would now be dead and you would be looking for another position."

Anthea could see by the surprise on her brother's face that he had not thought of this and after a moment he said grudgingly,

"It was certainly very quick-witted of you to remember to use the secret staircase."

"I was only just in time," Anthea said with a little tremor in her voice.

They did not speak again until they had arrived back at the Dower House.

Then Anthea ran upstairs, locked the door of her room, and flinging herself down on the bed, burst into tears.

She did not know why she was crying except that Harry was angry about everything that had happened and it seemed so sordid that Lord Templeton should have accused her publicly of being in the Marquis's bedroom.

She was not so obtuse nor so innocent as not to realise that the Social world would think that she had been behaving improperly.

She knew how upset her father and mother would have been and she found herself telling them both how she had thought what she did was for the best.

She had had no idea that this would be the result and Harry would be ashamed in the face of his friends gossiping about her.

She cried for a long time and, when Nanny came upstairs to knock on her door and see if there was anything she could do for her, she did not answer, but pretended to be asleep.

She did sleep for a little while later in the afternoon, but when it was time for dinner she felt that she could not face Harry and Charlie.

She knew inevitably that they would question her over and over again as to what had happened and perhaps would trip her up and realise that she had seen the Marquis more often than he had said she had.

Nanny brought her up something on a tray and later, when Harry came in to say good night, the room was in darkness and he tiptoed out without speaking.

But Anthea lay awake for a long time, thinking that whatever else happened at least the Marquis was safe and it was doubtful when he went back to London whether she would ever see him again.

*

The following morning, which she knew was the day of the Derby, she came down to breakfast to find as she half-expected that Harry and Charlie had already left.

"You never heard such a commotion!" Nanny exclaimed when Anthea looked into the kitchen to tell her that she was downstairs.

"What has happened, Nanny?" Anthea asked nervously.

"A footman arrived almost at the crack of dawn to tell Master Harry that his Lordship wanted him and Major Torrington to go to the Derby Meeting in his place because he felt unable to do so, so that they could report to him how his horse ran."

"Go to the Derby!" Anthea exclaimed in astonishment.

This was something that she certainly could not have foreseen.

"They went off as if they were competing in the race themselves," Nanny said, "and his Lordship sent one of his own phaetons for Master Harry to drive, so he was like a schoolboy, jumping for joy at the thought of it."

Nanny spoke almost scathingly, but Anthea knew from the expression on her face that she was very proud that Harry should be representing the Marquis and driving to the races in style.

As Anthea sat down at the dining room table to eat the egg that Nanny a few minutes later put in front of her, she knew that this would certainly alleviate Harry's anger.

She thought it was very clever of the Marquis to think of anything that would so quickly take his mind off what Lord Templeton had said at White's.

'Whatever happens, Harry must not attempt to fight a duel about it,' Anthea told herself, as she had last night.

She was certain that Harry would not be as good a shot as Lord Templeton, who would, like most of his generation, have fought a number of duels in his time and might wound Harry or even kill him.

'The Marquis must prevent it!' she thought frantically and then found it impossible to eat any more.

She went into the drawing room wondering if while Harry was away she dared go up to Queen's Hoo and ask to see the Marquis.

She wanted to talk to him, she wanted him to explain to her the answer he had to Harry's question, as he had promised he would have.

Then she supposed that she would have to wait until Harry's return and she doubted if, clever though the Marquis was, he could prevent the members of White's and everybody else to whom the story had been related from repeating what Lord Templeton had said.

She felt her face burn with embarrassment that she should have been thought to behave like Milly or the other members of the Marquis's house party of whom Nanny had spoken with such scorn.

Because it upset her so much to think about it, she sat down at the piano and in music expressed how shocked and disturbed she was.

She must have been playing for quite a long time, when the door opened and to her astonishment the Marquis came in.

She was thinking of him while she played, when he was sitting in the window, in what had once been her father's bedroom, as she had last seen him.

Despite the fact that he must be still suffering from the effects of Spring Fever, he looked magnificent and, of course, in his own inimitable way, overpowering.

Now, as he crossed the drawing room towards her, immaculately dressed, his cravat tied in a new intricate style that she had not seen before and his Hessian boots shining, it seemed impossible to believe that he was the same man whom she had tended so recently when he was weak and ill, lying almost unconscious against his pillows.

She rose nervously to her feet and then, as the Marquis stood beside her, she said,

"Surely – you should not be – up so soon? How do you – feel? Are you – all right?"

"I feel extremely well," the Marquis replied, "and, as I expect you have learnt by now, I have sent your brother and Charlie Torrington away so that we shall not be interrupted while I talk to you."

"I did not – think that was the reason," Anthea said, "but I knew that it would stop Harry from being so – angry – and I thought it very – clever of you."

"And now I have to be clever in preventing Templeton from behaving like the unutterable bounder he is and hurting you."

"Can you – do that?" Anthea enquired. "I don't mind for myself – as I never go to London, but it will upset Harry."

"And quite rightly," the Marquis said. "That is why, Anthea, I have come here today to ask you if you will do me the honour of becoming my wife."

He spoke very quietly in a deep voice that Anthea had not heard him use before and for a moment she thought that she could not have understood what he had said or else it was some kind of strange joke.

Then, as her eyes seemed to fill her whole face, she whispered incoherently,

"Are you – did you ask me – to m-marry you?"

"I want you to marry me, Anthea," the Marquis said, "and you must be aware that if you are my wife, no one will believe the unpleasant interpretation Templeton put on the fact that you were saving my life from his murderous intentions."

There was silence until the Marquis declared,

"I am begging you to marry me, Anthea."

For a moment she stared at him and then turned sharply away to walk to the window that was just behind them to say in a voice that sounded stifled,

"No – no – of course not!"

"Why not?"

"Because – there is no need for you to – marry me – and I would never accept – anyone in such circumstances."

"Supposing – " the Marquis began softly and then he stopped.

"Turn around, Anthea!" he said in a different tone of voice from the one he had used before.

She turned reluctantly and he saw an almost stricken expression in her blue eyes and her lips were trembling.

"I know exactly what you are thinking," he said, "so I am going to explain to you what is the truth in a way that I think only you will understand."

As he spoke, he turned round one of the armchairs so that it was facing the piano and said,

"Sit down!"

It was an order and, because Anthea had lost her voice, she did as he told her.

Then he went to the piano, sat down on the stool and looked down at the keyboard before he said,

"Just as you have spoken to me in music, Anthea, I am going to tell you about myself and my story starts when I was a little boy of eight years old."

He ran his fingers over the keys and then the music that came from him was of the happiness and sunshine of a child who is loved and loves, who lives in a world, just as Anthea had, peopled with fairies, flowers, and animals which were all part of childhood's enchantment.

As he went on, the fairies changed to Knights dedicated to perform noble deeds and save those they loved and there was gallantry and courage in the music.

Anthea understood that, as he had grown older, the Marquis was very romantic and to him women were so beautiful and sacred that he revered them, as he revered his mother.

Now he was grown up and in love and love to him was the splendour and perfection of a beautiful woman to he had given his heart to.

Anthea knew from the music that he had composed melodies for her and they were poems set to music and that he longed to discipline and better himself to be worthy of anyone so exquisite.

Then sharply, like a dark cloud blotting out the sunshine, there came disillusionment.

The woman he worshipped had laughed at him scornfully, held him up to ridicule and the world, her world, laughed with her.

At first his sufferings were so poignant and so desperately unhappy that Anthea, listening intently, felt the tears come into her eyes.

It seemed impossible that any young man should suffer such cruelty, the cruelty of being ridiculed, humiliated and scorned.

Then, when he seemed to have reached the very depths of despair, his pride helped him back from destruction, a pride that told him that he would not be conquered and he would not be trampled into submission.

From that pride, like Phoenix rising from the ashes, came the strength to fight back, to ignore and then conquer by sheer willpower those who had hurt him.

Then, as the Marquis went on playing, Anthea could see him growing older, at the same time harder and more cynical.

Everything spiritual that had mattered to him in his youth was thrust aside and he sought the physical and the material and found, because he could manipulate that to his own ends, in a way it gave him satisfaction.

Where before he had worn an armour that in his imagination was dazzling silver so that he could help those in need, now he wore an armour to protect himself against the barbs and arrows of those who would hurt him.

It was an armour which isolated him from everything that was soft, gentle and tender and, where he had been hurt, he now hurt others and in the same way as he had been crushed and humiliated, he now reduced others to less than the dust beneath his feet.

It was the march of a conqueror, who had no care for anyone's sufferings, who stamped his enemies into the ground and was not concerned for his friends.

Anthea could feel the cruelty of it and she clasped her fingers together until the knuckles were white.

She shut her eyes to listen and she could see the Marquis as she had first seen him, dominating, overpowering, at the same time magnificent – a man of whom everybody was afraid.

Then, so gently and so softly that at first she was not really hearing it, there was the same music, the same melody creeping back that there had been when he was young.

When she was aware of it, she could also hear it intermingled with the same theme that she had played to the Marquis yesterday, when she had been telling him what was waiting for him outside in the sunshine.

There was her interpretation of the song of the birds, her way of describing the streams and flowers, her way of telling him he was wanted and how much he could do for those who looked to him for guidance.

Then beguilingly and glowingly with a magic that she could hardly believe came from a man's fingers, he was telling her, although it seemed incredible, how much she meant to him.

He told her how she had swept away the agonies of the past, the disillusionment, cynicism, humiliation and despair.

Instead she had given him the starlight and the moonlight, she was holding flowers in her arms and she was indivisible from the sunshine.

It seemed to Anthea as if she had stopped breathing because it was impossible for her to believe with her mind what she was hearing.

But the understanding sprang from her heart and her soul and she felt her whole being vibrate towards the Marquis as if he was calling her.

Then suddenly the music came to an end and, as he took his hands from the keys, he rose from the piano and instinctively, as if he commanded her to do so, Anthea rose too.

For a moment they just looked at each other, her blue eyes held by his grey ones so that she could not look away and could not even draw in her breath.

Then the Marquis held out his arms.

Afterwards she was not certain if he moved towards her or she ran to him. She only knew that his arms were around her and his lips came down on hers, holding her captive.

This was what she had been longing for, crying for last night and thought that she would never know again.

Then it was impossible to think but only to know that he was holding her closer and closer.

His lips became more insistent, more demanding, and the music that she could still hear joined them so completely that they were not two people but one.

She felt her whole being vibrate to the wonder and joy his kisses gave her.

The Marquis kissed her until the room whirled round them and they were free and flying through the sky towards the sun.

Yet they were still entranced by the magic of the sounds that came from them both, linking them in a melody that was too perfect even to be expressed.

At last, when the sensations the Marquis was evoking within her and the dazzling wonder of his kisses seemed too glorious to be borne, Anthea made an inarticulate little sound and hid her face against his neck.

"My precious, my darling!" the Marquis said in a voice that was curiously unsteady. "I knew you would understand."

"H-how could I know – how could I guess that you could – play like that?" Anthea murmured.

"I have never before allowed anybody to hear me play," the Marquis said, "because I knew that the music that I made was too revealing and too intimate for anyone to hear except, my sweet, you."

He held her closer still as he said,

"When I heard you playing in the Minstrels' Gallery on Saturday night, I thought that I must be dreaming, for never in my life had anyone's music moved me as yours did or spoken to me so simply and yet so clearly that I understood every feeling and every thought that lay behind it."

His lips were on the softness of her skin before he went on,

"Then when I saw you I was afraid."

"Why?" Anthea enquired.

"Because, my precious, I believed you to be who you told me you were, the daughter of a professional concert pianist and I did not believe it possible that I could worship you, as I wished to do – as my wife."

"I-I don't think I – understand."

The Marquis smiled before he said,

"There is no reason why you should. All that matters is that we should be married, my precious little love, as quickly as possible, not only because by doing so we can prevent Harry from taking his revenge on Templeton, but also because I want you! I want you now, this instant, and I cannot bear that we should be apart even for a day, even an hour."

His voice deepened as he went on,

"You are mine, Anthea. I have looked for you all through my life, but thought I should never find you and that you did not exist."

"But you are so grand – so important," Anthea faltered, "I would be – frightened to be your – wife in case I made mistakes – and you became bored with me."

"Do you think that is possible?" the Marquis asked. "When we can read each other's thoughts and you can tell me in music what is in your heart and soul and I can tell you what is in mine."

He spoke simply and then he said as he saw the answer in her eyes,

"How could we be bored with ourselves when we are one person, my darling one, as I am sure we have been before and will be again for all Eternity?"

He spoke gently as he asked,

"Now tell me what you feel about me."

"I love you – *I love you*!" Anthea said. "I have loved you – although I did not realise it – because you were so kind and so understanding – but I never believed it possible there was anyone in the world who would – understand what I was – saying in music."

"Not only in music," the Marquis answered. "I understand your soul and your heart, the thoughts in your clever little head, and the sensations you feel in your exquisite body. They are all mine, mine, completely and absolutely and no one shall take them from me."

Then he was kissing her again, kissing her more possessively, more demandingly, as if he was half-afraid that he might lose her.

But Anthea was not afraid, she only knew that her whole being was pulsating with the wonder he was giving her.

Once again he twisted her lips a little, as he had done the first time he kissed her and she felt the lightning streak through her and she thought it impossible for anyone to know such ecstasy and not die from the glory of it.

*

The Marquis and Marchioness of Eaglescliffe came down the stairs at Carlton House amid a cloud of rice and rose petals to climb into the phaeton decorated with flowers that was waiting for them outside.

As they did so, the crowd who had gathered on the railings began to shout,

"Good luck, Eagle!"

"The winner again!"

"Eagle!" "Eagle!"

The Marquis waved to them good-humouredly as he picked up the reins of his superb team of jet-black horses and moved off.

There were more rose petals, cries of, "Good luck!" "Long life!" and "God bless you!" from the guests seeing them off as they drove into Pall Mall, the groom perched up behind them on the small seat, grinning with delight.

Only when they were out of sight did Anthea say,

"Have we far to go? You have not told me where we are staying for our honeymoon."

"I want it to be a surprise," the Marquis answered, "and, my darling, no man could have a more beautiful bride with whom to start on his honeymoon which, where we are concerned, will last a lifetime."

Anthea gave him a radiant smile from under her high-crowned bonnet edged with lace, which seemed to make her beauty even more ethereal and sylph-like than usual.

The Marquis's eyes rested for a moment on her face before he was forced to attend to his horses.

Anthea moved a little nearer to him to put her hand on his knee almost as if she wanted to reassure herself that he was really there.

It was not surprising that she thought it could only be a dream, because they had been married at a breakneck speed that had left her breathless.

Everything had been planned by the Marquis down to the last detail and only he, as Anthea knew, could have swept her and Harry into a Wedding that would silence any unkind or cruel remarks that might be made about her.

Harry had explained to his friends in White's the real reason why Lord Templeton had been forced to flee the country and how Anthea had saved the Marquis's life.

Who would believe anything else, when she was married from the house of the Marquis's maternal grandmother, the Duchess of Melchester, whom everybody admired and respected and of whom it was said even the Prince Regent was afraid.

The Prince Regent himself had insisted on acting as Best Man to the Marquis in the Ceremony, which took place at St. George's, Hanover Square and the Reception afterwards was held at Carlton House.

"Please – must we be so – grand?" Anthea had begged.

But the Marquis had replied,

"Does it really matter to us, my darling, whether we are married grandly or, as we would both prefer, quietly in the Chapel at Queen's Hoo? But we have to think of Harry's feelings and what your father and mother would wish if they were alive and, of course, what our children will hear in the future."

He liked the way that Anthea looked shy as he spoke of their children and the faint flush that came into her cheeks.

He told himself for the thousandth time that no one could be so pure, so innocent, so absolutely perfect and yet be on earth.

He had known then that he was doing the right thing and, when he gave Anthea a necklace of diamond stars to wear at her Wedding, he knew that she understood that what really mattered to them both could be expressed only by the music of the stars, which they would hear together on their Wedding night.

Because she was so radiantly happy and because she loved the Marquis so overwhelmingly, when he turned round in St. George's Church to watch her come up the aisle on Harry's arm, she did not look down as convention required.

Instead, as she moved towards him, her eyes shone more brilliantly than the stars around her neck and their love seemed to radiate out from both of them so that many people in the congregation felt a sudden pricking of their eyes and an unexpected hoarseness in their throats.

"Are you not going to tell me where we are going?" Anthea asked now.

"I think you should have guessed by this time," the Marquis replied, "that there is only one place that is so deeply associated with us both and the awakening of our love that it seemed impossible to go anywhere else on our Wedding night."

"You don't mean – you cannot – " Anthea stammered, "that we are going to – Queen's Hoo?"

"But of course!" the Marquis replied. "I want to make love to you, my adorable wife, in the room where I first kissed you and where you twice appeared like a celestial being to save my life. The room where you nursed me back to health and told me as you played to me that you loved me."

"Did I – really do that?" Anthea asked.

"You told me that you loved me, as no one has ever done since my mother died," the Marquis said, "and I knew, because I loved you in the same way, that we could never lose each other. In fact I was prepared to kill anyone who would prevent me from making you my wife."

He spoke quite quietly, but Anthea felt her heart turn over in her breast and she knew that he loved her wildly, as she loved him.

Tonight in the room that had belonged to her father, the room that had meant more to her than any other room in Queen's Hoo, she would find a Heaven of happiness that was inexpressible except in music.

When they had finished dinner in the boudoir, which had been lavishly decorated with flowers, the Marquis had sat looking at her across the table and thinking it impossible for any woman to be more beautiful.

Because he wanted Anthea to himself, there had been no servants to disturb them.

He had waited on her and kissed her between each course so that they neither of them had any idea afterwards what they ate or drank, except that it would only have been the nectar and ambrosia of the Gods.

"It is wonderful to be here with you," Anthea said softly.

"I hoped you would feel like that," the Marquis replied. "But because I want you to love my own home even more than this and perhaps we will not be coming here very often, I have an idea."

"What is it?"

"That we ask Harry to move into Queen's Hoo and look after it for us and when he marries we will give it to him as a Wedding present."

For a moment Anthea was speechless and there were tears in her eyes as she said,

"How can you – think of anything – so – so marvellous?"

The Marquis rose from his seat, walked towards the *Sèvres*-decorated piano and sat down at it.

"There is just one more thing I want to tell you, my darling," he said.

He started to play a song of love that not only drew Anthea's heart from her body, but at the same time, because there was an undercurrent that she had never heard before, she felt a wild excitement moving through her veins, up into her breasts and from her breasts into her lips.

She wanted her husband, she wanted him to kiss her, she felt as if her whole body ached for his hands on the softness of her skin and the beating of his heart.

Then, as the long song ended in a crescendo of notes, as if he knew what she was feeling and he felt the same himself, he rose to sweep her up into his arms.

She raised her lips, waiting for him to kiss her, but instead he carried her from the boudoir into the Master bedroom next door.

There were no candles alight, but the curtains had been pulled back and she could see the evening stars coming out overhead and just the faint glimmer of gold as the sun sank into the darkness over the corner of the world.

Then, although she could hardly realise what was happening, the Marquis had undone the negligée she had worn over her diaphanous nightgown and had lifted her into the great bed.

For a moment her eyes were raised to the stars and she was dazzled by them and then she felt as if they had moved into her body so that they vibrated and shone inside her.

She knew as the Marquis joined her and she felt the touch of his hands that the stars were in him too.

Just for a moment he held her very close, not moving, not speaking, but waiting as if the curtain was going up and something wonderful was about to happen.

Then very softly he said,

"I love you, I adore you, I worship you, Heart of my Heart, my star, mine, whom I shall never lose!"

"I-I love you!" Anthea breathed. "Please – darling – teach me about love – so that you will not be disappointed – or I shall fail you in any way."

"How could I be disappointed or fail myself?" the Marquis answered. "You are me, Anthea, and I am you, and now, my darling, I am going to carry you up into the sky so that you touch the stars and hold them to your breast and know that we are no longer human beings but as Gods."

As he spoke, Anthea felt as if the music from the spheres were playing behind his words and that, as he had said, he was carrying her up to the stars.

But the stars were already within them, the light of them dazzled her eyes and the music she could hear within her was the song of angels.

Then she became, as the Marquis had promised, one with him and their happiness was not human, but Divine.

OTHER BOOKS IN THIS SERIES

The Barbara Cartland Eternal Collection is the unique opportunity to collect all five hundred of the timeless beautiful romantic novels written by the world's most celebrated and enduring romantic author.

Named the Eternal Collection because Barbara's inspiring stories of pure love, just the same as love itself, the books will be published on the internet at the rate of four titles per month until all five hundred are available.

The Eternal Collection, classic pure romance available worldwide for all time.

Printed in Dunstable, United Kingdom